ALTERNITECH

ALTERNITECH

KEVIN J. ANDERSON

WordFire Press
Colorado Springs, Colorado

Cover design by Janet McDonald

Cover artwork image by Daniel Tyka

Kevin J. Anderson, Art Director

Book Design by RuneWright, LLC
www.RuneWright.com

Published by
WordFire Press, an imprint of
WordFire, Inc.
PO Box 1840
Monument CO 80132

Kevin J. Anderson & Rebecca Moesta, Publishers

WordFire Press Trade Paperback Edition September 2016
Printed in the USA
wordfirepress.com

Introduction

Science fiction isn't just a literature of ideas. Any good writer follows the consequences of those ideas, asking the next question, and the next, and the next. The five stories in this sequence all center on "Alternitech," a company that sends prospectors into alternate, similar timelines in order to exploit the differences. Imagine the small fluctuations in your day, how a few inches or a few miles-per-hour during a skid on an icy road could make the difference between a fender-bender and a fatal accident. Tiny changes like this could lead to a world where the Beatles never broke up, or where Lee Harvey Oswald wasn't gunned down after the Kennedy assassination, where an accidental medical breakthrough offers an unexpected cure to a rare disease.

Kevin J. Anderson

But a story isn't "about" that. It's about how those changes affect the people who witness them.

Music Played on the Strings of Time

He arrived, hoping to find a new Lennon, or a Jimi Hendrix. Or an alternate universe where the Beatles had never broken up.

As the air ceased shimmering around him, Jeremy staggered; with his head pounding, he sucked in a deep breath. His employers at Alternitech always made him empty his lungs before stepping through the portal. The company had strict rules limiting the amount of nonreturnable mass shuttled across timelines, even down to the air molecules. Take nothing tangible; leave behind as little as possible.

The air here smelled good, though; it tasted the same as in his own universe.

He snatched a glance around himself, making sure that no one had seen him appear. It had rained recently, and the ground was still wet. Everything about this new reality appeared the same, but each timeline had its subtle differences.

Jeremy Cardiff simply needed to find the useful ones.

•　○　•

The Pacific Bell logo on the phone booth had the familiar design, but with a forest-green background color instead of bright blue. He had always found a phone booth in the same spot, no matter which alternate reality he visited. Some things must be immutable in the Grand Scheme.

Jeremy reached into the pocket of his jacket and withdrew the ring of keys. One of them usually worked on the phone's coin compartment, but he also had a screwdriver and a small pry bar. His girlfriend Holly had never approved of stealing, but Jeremy had no choice—in order to spend money in this universe, he had to get it from somewhere here, since he could leave none of his own behind.

The third key worked, and the coin compartment popped open, spilling handfuls of quarters, nickels, and dimes—Mercury dimes, he noticed; apparently they had never gotten around to using the Roosevelt version. He scooped the coins out of the phone booth and sealed them in a pouch he took from his pack. Never get anything mixed up, the cardinal rule.

Time to go searching. Jeremy picked up the phone book dangling from a cable in the booth and flipped through the yellow pages, hunting for the nearest record store.

Before he had left his own timeline that morning, everything had happened with maddening familiarity:

"Your briefing, Mr. Cardiff," the woman in her white lab coat had said. The opalescent Alternitech: Entertainment Division logo shone garish on her lapel, but she seemed proud of it. Her eyebrows were shaved; her hair close-cropped and perfectly in place; her face never showed any expression. This time Jeremy saw she was attractive; he had not noticed before. Every other time he had been too preoccupied with Holly to notice.

"You tell me the same thing every trip," Jeremy said to the Alternitech woman, shuffling his feet. He felt the butterflies gnawing at his stomach. He just wanted to get on with it.

"A reminder never hurts," she said, handing him the high-speed tape dubber. It had eight different settings to accommodate the types of music cassettes most often found in near-adjacent timelines.

At least the woman had stopped giving him the "time is like a rope with many possible strands" part of the speech. Jeremy was allowed only into universes where he himself did not exist at that moment; it had something to do with exclusions and quantum principles. He chose never to stray far from his own portion of the timestream, stepping over to adjacent threads, places where reality had changed in subtle ways that might lead to big payoffs in his own reality.

Other divisions of Alternitech sent people hunting for elusive cures to cancer or AIDS, but they had been by and large unsuccessful. A cure for cancer would change history too much, spin a timeline farther and further away from their own, and thus make it harder to reach.

'Ghost music,' on the other hand, was easy to find. Jeremy wanted to find new work by Hendrix or Morrison or Joplin, a timeline where these stars had somehow escaped freak accidents or avoided suicide.

"Do you have everything now?" the woman asked him.

"All set." Jeremy stuffed the tape dubber in his shoulder pack. "I've got my money bag, a snack, some blank tapes, and even a bottle to piss in if I can't hold it." Sometimes the precautions seemed ridiculous, but he wasn't here to question the rules. Alternitech would deduct from his own commission the transport cost for every gram of mass differential.

"You have five hours until you return here," she said. The portal opened, shimmering inside its chrome framework. "I trust that will be enough time for you to search."

"I've never needed more than two hours, even if I have to walk to the mall."

She ignored that. He was disrupting her memorized speech. "You are entitled to your commission on whatever new music you locate, but according to our contract we retain all rights and royalties." She smiled. Her lips looked as if they had leaped off the screen from the Rocky Horror Picture Show.

"Of course," he said. He had already learned that once, with his first big payoff, finding three new albums by Buddy Holly—he had actually been looking because of Holly's name, and he had been so surprised he had almost forgotten what to do. Almost. He had coasted on the triumph for a year, but he had found nothing new in a long time. He felt the anticipation building each time, wondering what he might find.

Exhaling the air in his lungs, Jeremy went sailing into the timestream.

●　○　●

Shopping malls had to be the most ubiquitous structures in creation. Jeremy had never encountered a timeline where the mall did not exist.

Inside the record store, Jeremy scouted down the aisles. The new releases displayed the appropriate Big Hits; a familiar Top 40 single played on the store's stereo system. The important changes would be subtler, difficult to find.

He checked under the Beatles first. At other times he had found strange but useless anomalies—a version of Abbey Road that did not include "Maxwell's Silver Hammer," a copy of the White Album that actually listed the songs on the back, a release of Yesterday and Today that had retained the disgusting butcher shop cover censored in the U.S. But since he could not take anything physical back with him, cover variations were worthless. In this store, however, everything looked the way it should have.

Disappointed, he next tried Elvis, the Doors, Led Zeppelin, John Lennon—those would net him the most commission if he brought an undiscovered treasure back.

He might as well have stayed home.

With a sigh, he finally searched for Harry Chapin and Jim Croce, Holly's favorites. New songs by these two wouldn't sell well back in his own timeline, but he always checked, for her. He stopped himself—it didn't matter anymore. Who gave a damn for Holly? But he looked anyway.

He thought of Chapin, killed in a car accident … his Volkswagen smashed under a truck, wasn't it? And Jim Croce, dead in a plane crash at age 30, two weeks after his song "Time in a Bottle" had been a theme in a TV movie: She Lives, one of those oh-so-typical "my lover is dying of a terminal disease" films of the early seventies. Jeremy considered the song sappy and sentimental; Holly insisted it wasn't.

"You know, if it were me saving time in a bottle," he had said to her, "I could think of a lot better things to do with it. Like find more time for my own music."

He knew just how to push Holly's buttons. After one fight, he had left a box on her doorstep for her to keep "all those wishes and dreams that would never come true." He had intended it to be ironic; she had called it cruel.

He and Holly had such different needs that they clashed often over the two years they had been together, coming close and drawing apart. He decided it was probably over now for good. Jeremy had his music, his need to write songs and work toward breaking into the business. Holly, though, just wanted to hang out with him, wasting hours in conversation that had no topic and no purpose. She said it brought them together; he resented her for draining away time that he could have used for composing.

In the house he kept his own mixer, a MIDI sequencer, synthesizers, music editing programs, a set of panel speakers mounted on marble blocks and an amp that could lift the house two inches off its foundations if he decided to crank the volume. He had all the gadgetry, he studied the hits, tried to come up with a sure-fire blockbuster. Listening to the crap on the radio, he couldn't see that his own stuff was any worse.

He just needed a break. You had to know a name, get under the right label, and somebody would make your songs hits, crowbar you to the top of the charts. Otherwise, music people tossed unsolicited demo tapes out the window. Reject. Sorry, kid.

But Jeremy planned to get in through the side door, to make a name for himself by bringing 'ghost music' back to his own timeline and taking credit for it. Then the studio execs would be ready to listen to his stuff....

But it wouldn't happen here, not in this timeline, not in this record store. Jeremy sighed. No Beatles, not even any new Chapin. He flicked his gaze down to Croce.

Holly disagreed with Jeremy's approach to songwriting. She worked as a nurse and sometimes treated him like a patient with psychological problems. Therapy. Pop psychology. "You can't just find a formula and imitate it. You need the depth, the emotion. And you can only get that by drawing it from yourself, by being brave enough to look deep. But you're afraid to. You need to have something inside yourself before you can share it with anyone else."

But he knew Holly must be wrong. What did a nurse know about music? He played in bars on weekends, drawing a few crowds. Holly herself came to watch, sitting at a table near the stage and mouthing the words to his own lyrics that no one else recognized. Somebody would notice him. One of his songs would catch on. He needed a foot in the door and some more practice.

Startled, he found five different cassettes with Jim Croce's name on the side. In his own timeline, Croce had made only two albums, and most of those cuts had been compiled into varied "Greatest Hits" collections. After a moment of excitement—Jeremy always felt his skin crawl at finding an obvious change—he picked up the cassettes, glancing at the titles, reading the package copy.

In this reality, Croce's plane had never crashed. In the late 70s he had changed his style dramatically, but the cassettes didn't seem to be big successes. Croce had gone for dance music, funky R&B, with more and more desperate attempts at reaching the top 40 again. Songs like "The Return of Leroy Brown" were sure danger signs of waning creativity. On his last album Croce had not even written his own material, instead doing covers of old hits. When Jeremy found "Time in a Bottle: Disco Remix" he couldn't stop from chuckling.

Personal zingers aside, the alternate Jim Croce would have little commercial value for Alternitech back in his own timeline. And Holly would hate him for bringing this stuff back, for spoiling the memories. That would be too petty. He couldn't do that to her.

Not knowing quite why he didn't want to rub her face in it, he decided against the cassettes. Alternitech wouldn't be impressed anyway, and it would be a poor shadow to those new Buddy Holly tapes he had found. Better to leave old Jim dead in his plane crash. Jeremy shook his head, feeling pleased about completing his good deed for the day.

Then he noticed another tape shelved under "Misc. C." It bore his own name: JEREMY CARDIFF—This One's for Holly.

●　○　●

He paid for the cassette by stacking up the quarters from the phone booth, one dollar at a time.

The clerk looked at him strangely for paying in coins, but Jeremy was already tearing the cellophane wrapping from the tape case. The blurb sticker said "Contains the SMASH hit For Holly!" Promo material tended to exaggerate the magnitude of any song's success, but he felt enthralled that something of his had actually been called a hit.

By the time he emerged into the scattered crowds wandering the mall walkways, Jeremy had popped the cassette into his player. He sat down in one of the mall lounge areas, closed his eyes next to a trickling fountain, and listened.

Jeremy recognized the first two cuts as variations—sophistications, actually—on songs he had already written. The third cut was one he had just begun in his own timeline. He felt a sense of unreality drifting over him, euphoria at having achieved his dream. In at least one timeline he had succeeded. He wondered what his alternate self was doing now, how he was planning to follow up a successful first album—

Then the other part of it struck him with a force great enough that he sat bolt upright on the padded bench. He shut off the player. He could not enter another timeline where he himself still existed. Exclusion principles. The Jeremy Cardiff in this reality—the one who had been a hit musician—must be dead!

He checked the copyright date on the cassette liner. Last year. His counterpart must have died not long ago.

Jeremy had never dared to check before, had never been interested to find out what altered circumstances had erased his own existence in these other timelines. But here he had achieved his best goals, his dreams— what had happened to him? Another pointless plane crash like Jim Croce's?

Jeremy checked the timer that would send him back through the portal to Alternitech. He had three hours to find out.

• ○ •

"But can you tell me how he died?" Jeremy tried to keep his voice calm on the telephone. The record company receptionist had kept him on hold long enough that he had already needed to plunk four more quarters into the pay slot.

"Self inflicted," she said. Record company receptionists must go to school to learn that perfect 'go screw yourself' attitude, he thought. "You know, the old couldn't-handle-success story."

Jeremy's heart caught in his throat. Self inflicted? "Don't you have any other information? Please, this is important."

"Look," she answered, clearly impatient now, "he took sleeping pills, or shot himself in the head. I can't remember. Jeremy Cardiff had one hit, he made a little money, now he's dead. So what? The price of gas hasn't changed."

Jeremy swallowed as he hung up on her. "No, I don't suppose it has."

•　O　•

While waiting for a bus, Jeremy used the high-speed tape dubber to copy This One's for Holly onto a blank cassette from his own timeline, one he could take back with him. He would have to discard the original before he returned through the portal. The sky overhead was gray, as if preparing to rain again.

He listened to the rest of the tape after he had found a seat on the bus and sat back. He munched on a granola bar from his pack, careful to stow the empty wrapper back in the zipper compartment.

As the songs played, the initial astonishment wore off, and he began to hear his music with a fresh ear, like a listener would. Sadly enough, he was forced to admit that the songs seemed rather empty, the "oooh, baby, baby, yeah!" kind he had always scorned. Had he been too close to them? How could he have missed it? None of them had any punch.

Until the last song, "For Holly," which stood head and shoulders above the rest of the cuts. This had been the reason for the album. This had been the demo somebody had noticed.

He couldn't put his finger on the difference here— the music, the quality of his singing voice, the words? The pain sounded real. Somehow, it combined into a punch of emotion the others had lacked. He rewound the tape and listened to the song again.

When the bus stopped, he got out. The library was three blocks away.

●　○　●

He flipped through eighteen back issues of Rolling Stone until he found his own obituary. It occupied a quarter of a page, showing the cover of his album and his photograph. Jeremy felt an eerie chill seeing his own face stare at him from a photo he did not remember ever having taken.

The uncredited obituary stated the facts and little else. It carried the distinct flavor of an "also ran" notice. Jeremy Cardiff had had one hit, reaching #23 on the charts. He had been unhappy with his modest success, ended up washing down a bottle of sleeping pills with a pint of Jack Daniels. He would be sorely missed, but by whom it did not say.

"That's it?" He blinked up from the pages of the magazine, looking at the other people around in the library. No one noticed him, no one knew who he was. "That's all?"

He left his original cassette on the table in the library, hoping that someone would pick it up and listen to it.

• O •

During their last fight, Holly had said, "I hope you do become famous. I really do. Because I love you." Her voice was low with an undertone of exhausted anger, as it always was after the shouting stopped and they had both gone to their separate corners. "But you won't make room in your life for anything else. It doesn't have to be that way."

She tugged her blond hair behind her ears, keeping it out of the way. Faint mascara tracks marked her tears. Few people even recognized that Holly wore makeup, but Jeremy knew she spent half an hour each morning carefully constructing that impression.

"You'll never understand it," Jeremy said. He had tried to explain it over and over to her, but still she refused to give him the space, to let him have the time and energy he needed to devote to creating music. Instead, she was like a sponge, demanding his devotion, wrestling his attention to her own personal needs instead of to his composing.

"This isn't just a job like being an auto mechanic—" or a nurse, he did not add, "I really have the power to move people. I can send out a message that could make everyone think. But I have to take time to get it just right. I can't just drop what I'm working on whenever you're feeling insecure." The anger crept into his voice once more.

But Holly was having none of it. Quietly, she picked up her purse and went to the door. "Take all the time you need. Follow your yellow-brick road. I don't want to be the one responsible for you not achieving your dream."

He couldn't think of anything to say in response before she closed the door behind herself. He stood alone in his studio with the tall speakers, the amp, the MIDI equipment, and all his unfinished music. The house was very quiet.

•　○　•

He listened to his copy of the tape as he made his way back to where the return portal would open for him. He treasured the song "For Holly." *Would I want to go through time with you? Are you the one?*

What if he had given up everything with Holly for a chance that was ultimately a flop? What if practice and brute strength and determination were not enough? That was the way to manufacture songs, like the empty derivative stuff on the rest of his album. Listeners could see right through that facade. He could never send a message to the world if he had nothing to say.

As he walked along the road, Jeremy removed the last quarters from his money pouch. Since he couldn't take them with him, he tossed them in one big handful into a puddle in the gutter. Like a wishing well—but he no longer had any idea what to wish for.

He needed the substance inside himself before he could put it into the songs, but he had tried to bypass that part, to skip an important step. Sorry, no shortcuts allowed. With a sinking feeling he knew it would be a hell of a lot more difficult.

As he stood in position and waited, Jeremy listened to the last song on the tape one more time. He had managed the true inspiration once, and he could do it again. He could use "For Holly" as a model—and it would be a great gift for her. He must swallow his pride, tell her he had been stubborn.

His chronometer showed only a minute or so before he would return to Alternitech. The executives would be upset when he returned empty-handed again. But Jeremy felt anxious now, ready to start a new timeline of his own. He could get some studio to listen to "For Holly"; he could scrap the empty songs he was working on and spend the time he needed. Maybe Holly would even want to help him; he had never let her actually help him before.

Jeremy froze with his hand on the cassette player. He was not, after all, returning empty-handed. He had his own music—and the contract stated that any songs he found in alternate realities belonged to Alternitech/Entertainment. Everything. The whole copyright, hook, line, and sinker. He had signed it, knowing full well what it contained. If he tried to cross them, they would press the legal buttons and swallow him up.

He could not let that happen to a song like this. He had only one choice, but there was no use crying about it—Alternitech would deduct for the mass differential of a fallen teardrop left behind. He felt his throat trembling as he pushed the button.

The cassette made a thin whimper as it zipped through the high-speed dubber, sending his music back into nothingness, erasing it forever.

Even if he could remember the tune, the words, he could not copy the emotion that had made the song so powerful. Such things could not be imitated; they had to be felt. He didn't want to end up with a minor hit he could not repeat. He had to learn how to do it, not how to copy it.

The air shimmered in front of him, opening into a brief doorway back home. His chest felt like lead, but he exhaled, pushing the foreign air out of his lungs. Shifting his pack on his shoulder, he stepped into the portal.

Reality changed subtly around him. It was all right, though. He had new inspiration, new work to do. He opened his eyes in his own timeline.

It might not be the same cut he had heard on his own tape, but it would be different from his other attempts. His focus would be different. He had a song to write, for Holly.

Tide Pools

The return portal formed in the air like razor blades slashing through clear ice. Andrea stepped across the threshold, her mixed elation and disappointment so overwhelming that she barely noticed the skin-fizzing sensation of hopping back home from an adjacent timeline.

"I got something!" she called, unslinging the backpack from her shoulder. "How about a miracle cure for multiple sclerosis, anybody?" It wasn't what she had hoped to find, but she had to make it look good.

In the receiving room of Alternitech, portals and complex control panels surrounded her. At her announcement, technicians and other cure hunters began to pay attention. "How much follow-up do we need?" asked the chubby man in the operating booth.

"Not necessary—I got all the right data." Andrea brushed a hand through her short, sweat-rimed dark hair, feeling her cheeks grow warm.

Cure hunters like herself dreamed of such unlikely chances. Peeping into parallel timelines, digging through other-universe medical libraries, Andrea searched for effective treatments that doctors in her own timeline had somehow missed.

Who would have thought that a drug used for skin disorders would be amazingly effective against MS? When injected into the spinal columns of those suffering from the disease, the drug dissolved the small white plaques covering nerve sheaths.

No one in her own timeline had thought of it, but in an adjacent universe, a doctor had stumbled upon the treatment and published it to high acclaim. Alternitech would profit greatly from the discovery, and so would mankind.

The man in the operating booth spoke into his intercom, summoning verification reps to paw through her data. Other cure hunters applauded Andrea as they waited for their own gates to open. She surrendered her backpack and its contents to the security guard.

It was phenomenally expensive to haul foreign mass from other timelines. Hunters like Andrea recorded pertinent data onto the diskettes or videotapes they carried with them. Apparently, there was no cost to transfer information between timelines, though Andrea supposed the entropy specialists would probably come up with something sooner or later.

After the announcement of her discovery, the reporters would come, the television interviewers, the applause from the public, the heart-felt thank-you letters from MS patients given sudden new hope for their conditions. She allowed herself to revel in the times she made a find like this.

Andrea also felt a disappointment inside, despite the rewarding rush of success. After all, she had not been looking for a cure for MS. She had failed in her primary mission.

The problem gnawing at her was whether or not she should tell Everett. He was the one who had everything at stake.

•　○　•

Home at last, Andrea entered through the front door, propping it open to let in the fresh breeze. Sunlight gushed through the bay windows, warming the sunken living room.

Everett straightened from his work by the laser generator. "Andrea? Is that you?" She stood in full view, and he was staring directly at her. His eyesight grew worse every day.

"Expecting someone else to barge in and blow you a kiss?" she asked.

"I expected you home hours ago. Wait, I have to start all this up again!" He held up his hands, then felt his way around the equipment, squinting at it, careful not to stumble. "I have a surprise. Where are you? Come into the foyer—I've set that up as prime focus."

Andrea smiled to see him looking so earnest, so bustling. This was much better than the phase of moping he had gone through a month earlier. She went where he directed her and looked around the walls. Tiny faceted mirrors were mounted at strategic points around the room.

"Ta da!" Everett switched on his laser projector, and a 3-D holo sculpture congealed around her like a spider web of light, a kaleidoscope of rainbows. Each line was split, not quite resolved, so that it was really dozens of layered images overlapping each other, partially unfocused with chromatic aberration. His grids were out of phase, and she doubted Everett even knew it.

"My masterpiece," he said. "I wanted to leave something impressive behind. I call it Timelines. It's for you, Andrea."

Everett was looking at her with a childish expression of delight and anticipation on his face. His gaze was slightly off.

Timelines. She looked at the fuzzed edges of the light threads, the overlapping images that were almost but not exactly like each other. Perhaps it wasn't just some jittering lack of surety caused by Everett's fading eyesight and his trembling hands; timelines nearly overlapping but subtly different. He must have done it on purpose; she had to believe that, or else his failure would tear her heart apart. "I think it's beautiful, Everett. I don't know how you managed it."

He lowered his head to cover his smile. She almost expected him to say "Awww, shucks." Instead, he found a soft futon and sat down. "I was going to have it done by your birthday, but now everything takes me so damned long." He sighed. "Are you going to stay home with me tonight, or are you going back to Alternitech?"

Watching him made her wince her eyes shut. What good would a multiple sclerosis cure for him? She had failed him at the time he needed her most. She had to keep searching.

Heidegger's Syndrome. The disease selectively attacked the myelin sheaths around the optic nerve, then chewed away at the medulla oblongata, deteriorating the nerves that controlled breathing and heartbeat. After a slow descent into blindness, Everett would one day just find himself without a heartbeat, then fall over and die. Andrea dreaded the morning she would wake up to find him cold in the bed beside her. She could not prevent it in any way.

Andrea stared at Everett in the living room. The solution was painful and obvious. But Alternitech had flatly denied her permission to hunt among the timelines for a cure.

She walked up behind Everett, threw her arms around his waist, then pressed her cheek against his shoulder blades. The tapestry of light glittered around them, defeating even the sunlight. Timelines.

"It's your best work, Everett," she said. "I love it."

•　○　•

Andrea fidgeted in the university office of a man she had never met. In the halls of the Neurological Wing of the Deudakis Medical Research Facility, she could hear annoying sounds of construction, hammers and saws and power drills. She had had to weave her way around scaffolding and construction barricades to reach Dr. Benjamin Stendahl's office. The hall lights flickered, but remained on.

She looked at her watch again, sat down in the only uncluttered chair, then stood up once more.

Stendahl's computer sat on a corner of his desk, glowing with a garish screen saver of multicolored lines. She ran her fingertips along the spines of the journals on his bookshelves, stacks of dusty manuscripts, technical papers held together with old rubber bands; one band near the bottom of the pile had snapped, splaying curled printouts.

A man stepped into the office breathing heavily and mumbling to himself. He came to a full stop as he saw her. His eyebrows were like fluffy gray feathers mounted on his forehead. "Oh! I forgot." He dropped a bulging briefcase atop the stacked books on his desk. "You're here to talk to me about Heidegger's Syndrome—your husband, right? Well, there's nothing I can do for him. You realize how rare the disease is? Only eight people a year are diagnosed with it in all of North America."

Andrea thrust her chin forward. "I've read all your papers. Looks like you were making good progress toward a cure. Why did you stop work on it?"

"Simple answer—no more money. That's the rotten part. Heidegger's isn't really an insidious bastard like cancer or AIDS. Given some research data, I could do a lot. But our rhesus monkeys were rerouted and never arrived. I could afford only one grad student, but she got married and moved to Ohio. I couldn't get her replaced before the end of the fiscal year, when my funding went away."

Stendahl sat behind his desk, jiggling the mouse so that the screen saver dissolved to display a master menu. "I think 'orphan disease' is the colorful term they have for it. With research dollars so scarce, who wants to waste time coming up with a cure for something nobody cares about?"

"I care about it," she said. "Eight people a year care about it, and so do their families, and everybody they know."

Stendahl looked at her with sympathy in his big, dark eyes. "Look, millions of people get cancer, leukemia, cystic fibrosis. Heidegger's just doesn't cut it. The disease was a medical curiosity when it was first reported, little more."

Andrea stared at the journals on his shelves. Pounding hammers from the hallway punctuated her sentence. "And now?"

He shrugged again. "I'm working on other things."

●　○　●

Andrea wanted to spend her every waking hour hunting alternate timelines for a cure, but she needed to be with Everett. Each day was like Russian roulette with him, never knowing which heartbeat might be his last.

Seagulls wheeled overhead, tiny checkmarks that screamed against the booming rush of the Pacific. The ocean and the huge sky above made the universe seem oppressive in its grandeur. Headlands sprawled out in muted browns and grayish greens to the shore, where a string of tide pools dotted the wave-chewed rock like diamonds on a necklace. Barefoot and in cut-off shorts, Andrea and Everett picked their way among the rocks.

Andrea took sandwiches out of the pack, and they split a bottle of beer. Everett squatted beside one of the pools and dangled his fingers into the water, startling two crabs that ducked for cover beneath the rocks. He squinted to make out details. Eyeglasses would not help him; Heidegger's was not a problem of focus, but of the optic nerve itself.

The tide pools were colorful, filled with life, a microcosm of unfurled pale-green anemones, tiny fish, and shells. Snails worked their tedious way across the rock surface, finding rich patches of algae. Everett tossed a rock, watching the ripples spread to the boundaries of the tide pool, but constrained by the walls so that it could not affect the other tide pools.

"Each one is like its own universe," he said. "Full of life, nearly identical to the others, but different. "I'm like an anemone in a tide pool, stuck to the bottom, waving my fronds in the hope that I'll catch something, but ultimately trapped right where I am. You, on the other hand, are more like one of those rock crabs. With Alternitech, you can scuttle over the wall and get to other tide pools, go see new places, look at what they've got, and maybe take something back with you."

Andrea didn't know what to say. She did indeed have the flashy, high-paying career. Who could imagine a world where a "research librarian" was considered a glamorous profession? Andrea was constantly being interviewed, receiving awards and applause. She had loved it—until the search had become personal, and desperate, and she had failed.

"I'm still looking for something to help you. I'll find it. Don't worry."

A wave curled against an outcropping partly out to sea, dashing spray into the air like tiny crystal droplets. Two gulls swooped down, then wheeled high overhead.

"Why help me when you can help thousands?" Everett said. His voice held a strong resignation that had emerged from his initial depression.

"As if one cure precludes another!" Andrea scowled. "Why do we pit the two types of research against each other, as if they were our only two choices? The government spends more money maintaining flower gardens around monuments than they do on Heidegger's research—why does one bit of science have to siphon money from other science, rather than something else? Everything isn't equal." She looked down, though she knew he couldn't see her face anyway. "Besides, if I find something, I'll just tell Alternitech that I found it by accident while doing other research. They can't prove otherwise."

Everett smiled, like a parent watching a child deliver promises with false bravado, then he reached for his sandwich. She watched him squint until he found it.

She swallowed a large bite. "We should get back. I can go out hunting at least two more times today."

Everett's face was a plain mask of disappointment, but he said nothing.

•　O　•

In her long search, most of the alternate universes appeared identical. Digging into the medical research libraries, sometimes she discovered even less progress on Heidegger's Syndrome, or none at all. Twice, she found minimal successes beyond her own timeline, but nothing worth bringing back. With a run of unlikely bad luck such as Stendahl's, it seemed obvious that in some other timeline he would have received his rhesus monkeys, his grad student would have stayed an extra six months.

Throughout her search, she also had to find enough other tidbits to keep Alternitech happy. They had told her not to waste time hunting a cure for an orphan disease, yet they were delighted when she found a way to artificially change eye color from blue to brown and back again. Plenty of cosmetic and commercial applications, they said. Their priorities made her sick.

She had lost count of the timelines by now. On each mission, Andrea went directly to a university's medical library and buried herself in Stendahl's publications, checking to see if he had anything new to offer. This time, according to the library, Stendahl had completed his experiments, but his crucial summary papers were "in press," which meant they were not yet published and would be available only in his office.

Andrea hurried along the dim corridor. So far, every timeline had the same chaotic construction in the west wing of the building. Perhaps chaos itself was the only constant among the timelines. Yellow barrier tape blocked off corridors, light fixtures lay on the floor, the sounds of hammers and power saws echoed in the halls. Andrea passed a pile of new-cut boards, ducked under a scaffold holding drip-splotched cans of paint. She hadn't yet been able to determine if they were building something up or tearing something down.

Stendahl's door was closed. Taped to the wall beside his office hung a handwritten note giving an address to send Get Well cards. Under that, she read a newspaper clipping that described how Benjamin Stendahl had broken his leg after stumbling in a construction area, and that he was not expected to return to teach classes for the remainder of the semester.

Stendahl's door would be locked, but all cure hunters kept lock-picking tools in their packs. If this timeline had some crucial information for Everett, she would take whatever measures were necessary. As she worked at fumbling the slim tools into the door's keyslot, construction noises drowned out the sounds of her hidden efforts. But she kept looking over her shoulder. She was not good at this.

Wrapping her sweaty palm around the knob, Andrea finally opened the door. She ducked inside and closed it behind her, flicking the light switch.

Stendahl's abandoned office smelled oppressive and long-empty, though he had been in the hospital for only a week. She switched on the computer, letting it boot up as she scanned the bookshelves. She did not have much time to find what she needed, and Stendahl's cluttered organization made the task more difficult.

She saw the title on the fresh manuscript lying on top of one pile, then found a folder filled with memos, his hand-jotted records of the experiments, raw data. She flipped through the pages. At the end of his summary Stendahl even suggested a few treatment methods. "Yes!" she said.

She glanced at her wristwatch, trying to determine how soon the Alternitech portal would come back for her. She could use her camera to photograph each page of the hardcopy summary report, but this was raw data—files and files of it—experimental records, suggested follow-up tests. It would be laborious and time-consuming to copy all of it. More time than she had. But she could store everything onto one of her diskettes—if she could find the right files on Stendahl's computer.

Andrea went to the computer, glancing at the menu and searching for Heidegger files. As she feared, Stendahl had imposed little organization in his filing system. Some of the filenames contained the word "Heidegger," but when she called them up, they were mere memos requesting supplies. Stendahl had named seven of the files REPORT1, REPORT2 ... each taking up significant disk space. She checked the file-creation dates, then called up the most recent, but it had nothing to do with Heidegger research.

Out in the hallway, the construction workers used something that sounded like a jackhammer on the walls. Andrea tried to ignore the racket and concentrate on her work.

Finally, when she pulled up REPORT5, the words described all his tests, all his results, all his suggestions. Jackpot!

Excitement and anxiety growing within her, Andrea checked her watch again. She unzipped her pack and pulled out the various blank diskettes from her own universe. She pulled a disk out of its plastic sleeve and tried to slide it into the drive.

It was an eighth of an inch too wide. But she had other formats, other sizes to accommodate slight differences among the timelines. She tried another from her stack.

She finally found a diskette that fit. Stendahl's drive began formatting it. Alternitech experts had always been able to decode her diskettes, no matter how subtly different their computers might be. Of course, the techs might not help if she brought back something she had been instructed not to look for. She might have to call in all of the favors she had earned in her years working for Alternitech.

The disk finished formatting. It would take a few moments to copy the files. She didn't have much time; the portal would come back for her soon.

At the far end of the hall, one of the construction workers cursed as the jackhammer noise changed with an abrupt clank.

All the lights in the building went out.

Stendahl's office filled with blackness. The computer died. Andrea's hopes died with it.

•　○　•

By flashlight, she photographed as many pages of the draft manuscripts as she could. Working backward, Andrea snapped each image of conclusions, then the experimental method, and finally began plowing through all the raw data. She stared at her chronometer, watching the time tick down.

Alternitech's machinery cast her across the parallel universes at random like a fishhook in the water. Now that she had found a timeline that offered hope for a Heidegger's cure, chances were very slim that she would ever find herself back here. Frantic, she kept photographing the data, hoping that her flashlight provided enough illumination for the pictures to turn out.

Finally, when she could not wait a second longer, Andrea clicked one more photograph, then ran out of Stendahl's office, leaving the papers scattered all around. Glowing green EXIT signs shone in the darkness. She heard voices calling, complaining about the power outage. By the bobbing light in her hand, Andrea ran through the halls, dodging construction barricades. She had to get back to the portal.

A gruff voice yelled for her to bring the flashlight over so they could find the circuit panel, but she ignored it. She nearly tripped over a pile of pipes against one wall, but she caught her balance. Reaching the secluded stairwell, Andrea stumbled into the shadows just as the Alternitech portal slashed through the air.

Clutching her precious data, Andrea fell across the sea of timelines.

* O *

"Well," Stendahl said, raising his bushy eyebrows, "that's the good news." Andrea suddenly felt her stomach turn into ice.

He folded his hands on his desk and leaned toward her. Around him, she could see photocopies of the article and notes she had taken from the alternate universe. Stendahl had studied them, marked them with a red pen. She spotted several pieces of data circled, a few with exclamation points beside them. Andrea feared that she had not managed to include the one page that contained crucial measurements or descriptions of the one round of tests that would have allowed Stendahl to create a treatment for Heidegger's. It would all be lost.

Alternitech management had not been pleased with Andrea when she had returned with information on Heidegger's syndrome, information she had been specifically told not to seek out. They had suspended her, until they received a phone call from an angry senator whose daughter was even now being treated for multiple sclerosis—using the prescription Andrea had brought back. The phone call seemed like a miracle cure to her situation.

Now, Everett was the only one who had something to lose.

Andrea met Dr. Stendahl's gaze. "What is it?" she said, her voice hoarse. "What's the bad news?"

"I've confirmed—er, I mean I agree with my own conclusions." He forced a wry smile. "This research does indeed suggest a treatment regimen that could offer hope for people diagnosed with Heidegger's syndrome. But—"

Andrea flinched, but she didn't dare say anything else.

Stendahl looked away. "As with so many other ailments, beginning the treatment at the onset of the disease holds the key to the cure. If we could have started this right when your husband's eyesight was affected, when the disease was still confined to the optic nerve, we might have had a chance. He could have suffered a loss of eyesight, but the disease itself would be eradicated."

His feathery eyebrows rode up his forehead. "In your husband's case, the disease has already migrated to the medulla oblongata. The damage is already being done to the crucial nerves that govern involuntary functions such as heartbeat and respiration. This treatment itself purges the disease, but at the cost of destroying the nerves that are affected—somewhat like amputation."

Andrea took a long, shuddering breath. "Obviously, we can't do that in Everett's case. Not anymore." She felt a dry whispering sound in her ear, as of her own ragged hope draining away.

Stendahl was lousy at sounding optimistic. "From now on, anyone else diagnosed with Heidegger's will have a chance. You've saved those eight people a year you were so concerned about. No one else would have funded my research. You have that to show for your efforts, if nothing else."

Andrea found she couldn't listen any more.

•　O　•

Mist generators sent a cool fog toward the ceiling of the room, making the bright green and red laser beams stand out. Everett had been furiously working on another sculpture, fine-tuning it and trying to finish while he could still function. He had cranked up the laser intensity to the maximum safe level, just so he could discern the beams with his failing eyesight.

With the rest of the house darkened and only a few stars visible out the window, Andrea lay next to him on the floor, looking up at the laser tracery.

Everett spoke in the darkness. "There was a poet during the Boer War who said to live every day as if it were your last, for one day you're sure to be right."

"When did you start reading poetry?" Andrea said, trying to change the subject.

"I've had a lot of time to do things while you were off at Alternitech." He sighed. "But I'm glad you found the cure anyway."

"You're still going to die!" Andrea snapped. Her failure seemed like fluttering wings around her head.

"We're all going to die," he countered. "But you've given a longer life to the other people who get the same stupid disease I did." He took a long breath. "I came to terms with this illness a long time ago. It's you who need to accept it."

"I had to try," she mumbled. But she began to wonder if her obsession to find a cure, her need not to fail at the task she had set for herself, was actually more for herself instead of Everett.

"I know you did," he said. "Thank you for trying, Andrea. But all those days you were gone hunting ... I would rather have gone to the mountains with you, done a few more bed and breakfasts up the coast." Everett's words stung.

"There are plenty of other versions of me in other universes who will have a long and happy life with you. In our timeline, I had an unlucky break. I got an incurable disease that nobody's ever heard of. It just doesn't happen in this timeline, with this Everett and this Andrea."

He sat up abruptly. "We've got money saved, so why don't we spend it? Besides … you'll be getting a big life insurance check from me before long."

Andrea winced, but he gripped her hand. She thought of the hours she had lost in her desperate hunt. "I suppose I could take a leave of absence from Alternitech," she said haltingly, "especially now. It would give them time to cool off." She flashed him a smile that was at first forced, but gradually grew sincere as she thought of the things they could do together, now that all the restraints had been snipped away.

"All right," she said. "Let's go be alive as long as we can."

An Innocent Presumption

Afreak accident. Never happen again in a million years.

Rain slicked the pavement like a black mirror, reflecting the amber lights of the tow truck and the squad car's scarlet and blue flashers. A Toyota SUV had stalled high on the span of the Oakland Bay Bridge, angled so that it disrupted two lanes of traffic. Cars slowed across the bridge, crawling forward like a slow but belligerent garden slug.

A cop stood in the cold drizzle, waving his arms and fruitlessly directing traffic while a tow truck backed up, aligning itself to remove the offending

SUV. Its warning beeps sounded like high childish screams.

A placid-looking older man in a blue Mercury eased forward to change lanes and bypass the obstacle. The cop held up one hand and waved with the other. The blue Mercury lurched forward while cars in the adjacent lane struggled to stop.

A different driver jumped the gun and accelerated, then hit the brakes. He skidded forward on the slick road and crunched into the rear of the Mercury. With the impact, the older man's trunk popped open.

Disgusted, the cop walked forward, holding out both hands to stop traffic. The driver of the rear car rolled down his window to yell curses.

The older man in the Mercury opened his door, looked at the railing of the bridge high above the gunmetal-gray water. Dazed. Determined.

The frowning cop saw the young woman's bloody body in the Mercury's trunk. Two deep and brutal slashes across her face, her cheeks sliced open to expose white teeth. Both eyes ruined by the blade. Her throat cut all the way to the windpipe and spine.

The cop yanked out his service revolver, holding it in a stance he had often practiced at the firing range but never used in the line of duty. The old man froze before he could make a run for the edge of the bridge. The drizzle continued, but everything else had fallen silent, a snapshot tableau.

After two years and seven victims, intensive manhunts and giant budgets from crack crime-solving agencies, "Slasher X" was caught because of a silly fender-bender, a mere coincidence.

• ○ •

Another day on the job exploring alternate timelines.

Heather Rheims shouldered her pack, looking like a nondescript student. She wore a loose flannel shirt and comfortable jeans, a look that was in style in virtually every parallel universe. Timeline prospectors had to be unobtrusive, finish their tasks without drawing attention to themselves, then slip back through the portal to the central complex of Alternitech.

With her long rusty-brown hair and large gray-blue eyes, she passed as a typical college sophomore. Only her sharp gaze and hard expression revealed that she had scars and concerns beyond looking for parties at the student union or picking up guys in her poly-sci class.

Now, inside the main control room, portal frames gleamed in the too-white light. The air was always frigid, overly air-conditioned to pamper the dimensional equipment. One of her fellow timeline prospectors, a tall crewcut blond who looked as if he belonged in an ROTC recruiting office, came up to her. Rod's normally stony face was a mixture of sympathy and victory. "Hey, I hear they caught the bastard last night."

Heather's lips formed a grim line. She took a moment before answering to make sure her voice was steady. "Better late than never, I guess. Although if they'd caught him after victim number three instead of number seven, then I could still go biking on the headlands with my sister."

Rod squeezed her shoulder, then turned away as the tech supervisor called his name and prepared the portal for his day's assignment.

Heather said, "Still looking for novel leukemia treatments?"

"No, just novels." Rod gave a foolish smile. "Maybe Mario Puzo's sequel to The Godfather, or another historical epic by James Clavell. Maybe I'll find a universe where Stephen King never did retire." He went over to the dimensional doorway as the air shimmered and crackled with a smell of ozone.

Alternitech explorers like Heather sidestepped into parallel universes nearly identical with the modern world but with subtle differences: timelines where the Beatles had not broken up, where James Dean had a long and successful film career, where scientific researchers had achieved useful medical or technological breakthroughs that, for whatever reason, had been stymied in this world. A timeline prospector's job was to identify these differences and bring them back home, where Alternitech would sell them to the highest bidder.

"Oh, Ms. Rheims?" called the tech supervisor in his thick British accent. "If you would grace us with your presence, we are ready to send you."

With the news of Slasher X in all the papers, the tech supervisor didn't give Heather his usual deprecating smirk about her "embarrassing" current quest; since her patron paid a generous fee for Heather's skills, Alternitech allowed him his eccentricities.

"Money-Is-No-Object" Feldman was obsessed with the John F. Kennedy assassination. For over a month now he had sent Heather on expeditions into parallel universes in order to secure evidence that proved or disproved the conspiracy theory.

Now she shouldered her backpack, taking several deep breaths to prepare herself. She exhaled all the air, then stepped forward into the ripple—

—Without moving, she found herself in another universe that seemed identical to her own. She had three hours here, enough time to ransack the archives in the university library.

The city maps were similar in every timeline, with only the most minor deviations of street names. She knew exactly how to get to the UC San Francisco library or, failing that, the main downtown branch. For her purposes, all she needed was a microfilm archive or public access computers with newspapers dating back to 1963. Despite all the differences, the Windows Operating System seemed ubiquitous across timelines.

The routine was familiar by now. Heather even had her favorite carrel picked out. Sometimes, she had found greater evidence for a conspiracy, various shooters other than Lee Harvey Oswald; in some timelines, no assassin had ever been caught or even accused. In others, no crusader or conspiracy theorist like Jim Garrison had even raised the possibility, and Kennedy's murder went quietly into the history books as the work of a single madman.

"Money-Is-No-Object" Feldman was delighted with each nuance, each deviation, although so far the clues added up to nothing more tantalizing than the blurry photos often used to "prove" the existence of Bigfoot or the Loch Ness monster.

In this timeline, though, Heather felt a thrill as she discovered a significant change in history: This universe's Kennedy had survived the shooting, living out his term in office paralyzed from the waist down. After the assassination attempt, however, he had no longer been a fiery leader, and his presidency was remembered as basically ineffective. No shooter had ever been caught.

She followed the history threads, surprised at how easily the timeline's broad strokes had shifted back to her version of "normal." Heather used her hand scanner to copy the documentation. Feldman would be ecstatic.

Since she had a little time remaining before she needed to find her way back to the Alternitech portal, she glanced at current events. When she stumbled on the headline of the morning edition of the San Francisco Chronicle, Heather sat frozen, gulping the details with her eyes.

"Slasher X Claims Eighth Victim."

Then, of course, she knew exactly what she had to do.

●   O   ●

Parallel line after parallel line. Feldman's enthusiasm did not diminish as Heather continued to retrieve tantalizing nuggets that maintained the eccentric millionaire's funding. But she had another mission now. She no longer cared about the razzing from the tech supervisor or the other timeline prospectors who didn't consider her "tabloid work" to be worthy of Alternitech's potential.

Now, Heather was saving lives, innocent people just like her sister Janni.

In each new parallel universe, her first action was to check the newspapers, then make an anonymous phone call to tip off the police. The story was always the same: Her own parallel universe was the only one in which a bad-luck traffic accident had exposed the serial killer's identity.

When she delivered her bombshell of information, the detectives were sometimes skeptical, sometimes angry, other times mercifully grateful for any lead. Since the killer had been caught in her own timeline, Heather had followed the details of the case, and she could offer enough veracity to convince the investigating homicide detectives that she wasn't a crank.

She understood, for instance, that Slasher X—an older retired man with the unusual name of Eric Keric—used a fat black marker to draw an X on the faces of his victims before commencing the bloodier work. Keric slit the throats first so that the victims didn't struggle, and his thick carving knife could make precise strokes along the dark line he had marked, crossing out their faces. Many nightmares ago,

Heather had been called in to identify Janni's mutilated body—her face gashed with the terrible deadly X, her throat cut....

After a while, Heather stopped even checking the reports before she made her anonymous call. She simply tipped them off to Eric Keric and let the professionals handle it from there. It was so easy to be a good citizen, to get her revenge for Janni ... and to make sure that Slasher X paid the price for his terrible crimes. She began to feel like a hit-and-run crusader for justice, almost like Jim Garrison tirelessly trying to track down JFK's killers.

In her work for Feldman, she also came back in triumph to Alternitech. At last, she found a parallel line where Lee Harvey Oswald had lived long enough after being shot by Jack Ruby to blurt out a confession. With his dying breath, Oswald had fingered a man named Francis Tarryall, a shifty Dallas businessman with ties to Cuba and the Soviet Union. He'd been in trouble with the law many times but had managed to hire the best lawyers, to get evidence dismissed, and he had always walked. But after Oswald's accusation, Tarryall's trial was swift and the outcome sure. Tarryall never confessed, but the investigations by that universe's Warren Commission yielded seemingly incontrovertible evidence.

Heather copied several months of news stories so Feldman could study the aftermath.

She was rushed at the end because this time her usual call to the police had taken an excessive amount of time. The detective—not one of the familiar names usually assigned to the Slasher X case—asked too many questions, wanted to know about the killer's victims, pumped her for even the most obvious details.

Frustrated, she insisted that he check out Eric Keric, even divulging the old man's address, which she had memorized. The fact that the detective knew Keric's name and where he lived was a good sign. Perhaps the police had already been following him....

Rushed and exhilarated with her new Oswald discovery, Heather hurried back to meet the Alternitech portal. She promised herself a nice restaurant meal to celebrate a productive and satisfying day.

•　○　•

Alternitech prospectors rarely returned to the same parallel universe, but Mr. Feldman offered a substantial bonus. He had discovered with great glee that Heather hadn't obtained the full story about Francis Tarryall.

She'd copied later articles without reading them, and one of her last wire-service transcripts cast extreme doubts on Oswald's dying confession. Other evidence came to light that Tarryall and Oswald had been very personal enemies, their philosophies close enough that minor differences led to shouting matches and hatreds. Some of the Warren Commission's conclusions had begun to unravel … but Heather had not obtained the rest of the story.

She supposed that her patron wanted to seize any possibility that the conspiracy hadn't actually been solved. In his subconscious at least, Feldman perhaps needed something to hold onto. Her last mission had apparently given him the answer, but now he hoped she could cast doubt once again.

Heather stepped through the portal, backpack and equipment slung on her shoulder, and went right to work. The answer was obvious as soon as she scrolled through newspapers a few months farther ahead in time. Francis Tarryall was proven innocent, much of the evidence found to be false or misleading, Oswald's confession dismissed as a dying man's last vendetta with no relevance to the JFK assassination.

As she copied the articles, she recalled that this was the parallel reality where she had spent so much time arguing with the skeptical detective about Slasher X. Heather flipped through recent newspapers in the library, looking for headlines proclaiming that the killer had been caught, that innocent victims had been saved. She could take credit for the justice, but she alone would know it. This was her quest … just like Feldman's.

But she found no headline, no story whatsoever, no mention of Eric Keric or his arrest. The detective had ignored her! It was unbelievable.

With a fluttery dread, she flipped past several months and found no banner stories announcing the serial murders. Heather brushed her rusty-brown hair behind her ear, blinking in puzzlement. It didn't seem possible that Slasher X had managed to hide all of his victims, that people like poor Janni were simply written off as missing persons, runaways, unexplained disappearances … maybe even alien abductions.

What if, in this alternate timeline, Eric Keric himself didn't exist?

Breathing quickly, hoping that was the answer, she pawed through the residential phone book. In her own universe, Keric did not have an unlisted number. She found him right where she expected his name to be. The address listed was the same.

The bastard hadn't been caught. She had called the police, given her information—but the idiot detective had apparently done nothing, and the killer remained on the loose.

She looked at her watch. Still more than an hour left, since she had been so quick to get the answers Feldman needed.

Indignant, Heather thought about calling the detective again, demanding to know why he hadn't acted on her information. But she would not be coming back to this parallel universe, and if she didn't make sure that Slasher X was caught, then all his later victims would be on her conscience.

She could go there herself. She had never faced her sister's killer, never even seen the madman. Eric Keric had no idea who Heather Rheims was, despite the fact that she had turned him in timeline after timeline.

She made up her mind in an instant, even though in a horror movie this was probably a very bad decision. But Alternitech would sweep her away in an hour, no matter what happened. After all, Eric Keric had no reason to suspect her, or even recognize her. Heather decided to take the risk.

• O •

The murderer's house was repulsively charming and quaint. Neat bluechip junipers lined the walkway up to his little cottage. Flower boxes held green succulents and brown perennials that had died back for winter. Heather thought of the wicked crone's gingerbread house from the story of "Hansel and Gretel."

The front door was painted a slate gray with white trim. Obviously the old sociopath took time between killings to keep his house immaculate. She drew a deep breath and glanced at her watch again before knocking on the door. Only half an hour remained before the Alternitech portal would return. In her jacket pocket, she clasped a can of pepper spray.

Eric Keric had never seen her before in his life. She convinced herself she had nothing to worry about. Heather hoped that she looked like a newspaper salesperson or some other door-to-door annoyance. Then she rang the bell.

The old round-faced man pulled back the curtains beside the door and stared at her for an instant, then ducked away. Keric opened the door, and Heather stepped forward, tense and ready to lure him into a brief but incriminating conversation.

But his hand moved like a rattlesnake, snatching her long rusty-brown hair. "I'm not taking any more of this!" He yanked her head toward him. "And I've certainly had enough of you."

Before she could fumble the pepper spray out of her pocket, he swung the baseball bat that he kept beside the door, striking her a harsh sharp blow on the side of the head. Heather didn't even have time to cry out....

Pain hammered through the grogginess. She had been stunned into twilight for only a few minutes, but

Eric Keric had had enough time to drag her into the kitchen and thrust her into a metal chair beside the dinette table. He had lashed her elbows and wrists with two rubbery bonds—extension cords, she realized as she fought her way back to full awareness. Her ears rang, and bright colors swam at the fringes of her vision.

Keric dragged a thin wooden easel across the linoleum floor, standing it in front of her. He was dressed in a checked shirt, partly unbuttoned so she could see his low-necked undershirt and wiry gray chest hair. His sleeves were rolled up on his forearms as if he was ready to get down to work.

The smells and appliances in his kitchen, speckled Formica countertops and stainless-steel sink, were the trappings she had come to associate with kindly grandfathers, but Eric Keric seemed anything but paternal as he glared at her with both fear and anger in his eyes. He pulled the easel in front of her, and Heather lifted her throbbing head to look at it.

"I don't know who you are," the old man growled, "or why you keep tormenting me. What have I done to you?"

She tried to make words, but only a groaning sound came from her slack mouth and thick tongue. The ringing in her ears grew louder. He pulled up the white cover sheet on the easel's large sketchpad, and

Heather was astonished to see an accurate, painstakingly rendered pencil and charcoal sketch of her own face. Keric straightened the easel so that she was forced to look at herself. She wondered if she might be hallucinating.

"You … killed my sister," Heather finally blurted.

The old man scowled at her. "I didn't kill anyone—no matter what you keep saying, no matter what the police accuse me of." Heather couldn't figure out what he was talking about. "You are an evil, spiteful woman. I know you won't tell me who hired you, or who is responsible for this conspiracy, but you've succeeded in ruining my life—if that was your purpose."

He drew a deep breath, and his eyes flickered shut as if he were composing himself, then he squared his shoulders. "But I cannot change other people. I must change myself. I must take control of my life."

He turned away from her as if he couldn't bear to look at Heather's face. She knew she'd been stunned for only a few minutes at best. He couldn't possibly have drawn the exquisite portrait in that amount of time.

"The police have come to my house five times, twice with search warrants. They ransacked my private possessions, everything I own, but they found nothing, won't even tell me what they think I've done or what they're looking for."

Then he pointed an accusing finger at her. Heather was so frightened she tried to squirm away. The chair screeched with her movement, but she could not break the extension cords.

"Because of your harassment, I've lost my job. It wasn't much, but I worked hard at it. They had no reason to fire me." Keric paced the kitchen floor, and his face had a pathetically desperate plea written across it. "Don't you think every day isn't enough of a struggle? I walk on the edge, but I have the strength. I know how to deal with this burden...."

His voice became a low growl, and his eyes lit up. "But you keep piling more and more stress. You're trying to drive me over the edge. You want to push me into some violent action. I don't know what you have to gain by making me go ... berserk."

He clenched his fists but then squeezed his eyes shut again, breathing deeply as if reciting a silent mantra to himself. "But I won't let you. You don't have the power. My life is under my control. You cannot force me to break the law or to hurt anyone."

He withdrew a fat black marker from his pocket and wrenched off the plastic cap with a squeak. She could smell the ink's pungent sour fumes, and her heart skipped a beat. Slasher X always scribbled his indelible mark on the faces of his victims before he cut with the heavy knife.

"You have no power over me," he said, and turned.

With a brutal swift stroke and then a backwards slash, he made a black accusing mark across the picture he had drawn, crossing out her face, obliterating the sketched eyes as if he had eliminated her.

"There," he said, satisfied. "You can no longer bother me."

Keric tore the picture off of the easel and carried it, fluttering in his hands, over to a wooden closet door beside the refrigerator. On the back of the door, skewered on a long nail, hung a stack of sketches. Now, Keric stabbed Heather's portrait on top of the others, faces of men and woman, all of them X-ed out.

"Like all those others, you simply don't matter to me anymore."

Her thoughts spun with what he had said. Could it be true that in this parallel timeline Eric Keric had never become Slasher X? That he had found a way to divert his murderous rage and take it out symbolically on his sketches rather than using a knife? She felt sick.

And if this particular incarnation of Eric Keric also had deep psychological problems but retained his sanity by the thinnest of threads … then by making anonymous phone calls accusing him of crimes, had she driven the old man closer toward an edge he had so far managed to avoid?

He went behind her, and Heather was afraid he would strike her, cut her throat. But then she felt the extension cords tug at her elbows and wrists—and Heather found herself freed.

The old man tossed the cords onto the linoleum floor. "Go. Get out of here. You are erased from my life."

Heather stood, disoriented, still feeling the concussion. She looked at the old man, but couldn't say a word. Too many conflicting ideas clamored in her mind.

Bolting like a frightened rabbit, she ran for the front door. She had only a few moments before the Alternitech portal would appear. Keric stepped after her, not in pursuit, but eager to seal the door tight behind her. She looked over her shoulder. "I'm … sorry. I made an assumption, perhaps a wrong one."

She yanked open the door—and startled herself. She stood facing a carbon copy of Heather Rheims, another her. But this one held a handgun, drawn and ready to fire.

Heather's first absurd thought was that this version of herself had come more sensibly prepared than with a pocket can of pepper spray. She recovered and figured it out first. "Of course. There have to be Alternitechs in parallel timelines."

"Yes, and we both had the same idea," the other Heather said. "Did you kill him?"

Then Eric Keric stepped up, crestfallen and anguished. "Why won't you leave me alone?"

The other Heather's lip curled, and she swung up the handgun. She said accusingly to Heather, "Why did you let him live?"

"Because he … isn't guilty," she said. "Did you look for the headlines in this universe? Did you see any mention of Slasher X? Did the police react strangely when you called to turn him in?"

The alternate young woman kept the pistol aimed at Keric, but her expression wavered.

"This guy might be a brutal killer in most of the parallel universes we've visited, but not here. Oh, he's got plenty of mental problems, but so far he has managed to deal with them. He hasn't hurt anybody."

"That's ridiculous," said her counterpart.

"I know … but it's still true."

Keric looked back and forth between the identical young women, resigned instead of surprised. Heather realized that an endless succession of parallel versions of herself had come here to accuse him.

"This one doesn't kill people," Heather insisted. "He just draws pictures."

"How can I accept that?" said her alternate. "I need to do something for Janni. This was my only chance for revenge. How can I let that go?"

"Would I lie to you?" Heather looked at her with a deeply sincere expression. And then the other part of the puzzle slammed into place with thunderous force. "And in this timeline, Janni must still be alive."

Before she could continue the argument, before she could hope to see her sister again, the Alternitech portal shimmered in the air. Heather looked at her counterpart, who wore a startled expression on her face probably identical to her own.

But she couldn't stay. The portal beckoned. She knew she was not likely to come back to this parallel universe ... and she had wasted her time here. Heather had no choice but to return, without seeing Janni again.

But perhaps her counterpart would use her time for something more beneficial than useless revenge.

•   O   •

When she returned, blinking and disoriented, Heather stepped out of the portal into the Alternitech control room. Quickly, the tech supervisor and two security men came up to surround her. Heather didn't know what had gone wrong, why they were so intent on intercepting her.

"Ms. Rheims," said the tech supervisor, "kindly hand over all of your documentation on the John F.

Kennedy assassination. Your investigation is now terminated, your information forfeit."

Heather shrugged off her backpack, her mind spinning in another direction. She hadn't even thought about Feldman and his obsessive quest. "What's wrong?" She removed all her scans and copies about the frame-up of Francis Tarryall, how the JFK conspiracy remained unresolved. "I found some interesting information, but—"

"Mr. Feldman apparently deceived us and has cost Alternitech a great deal of money. He defaulted on his last several payments, and we've just discovered that he's bankrupt."

"Bankrupt? Money-Is-No-Object Feldman has no money?" She tried to wrap her mind around that shift in reality.

With his sarcastic British reserve, the tech supervisor looked at her. "Mr. Feldman insists it's a conspiracy designed to prevent him from discovering the truth about the JFK murder."

Heather felt numb. Somewhere, in another universe, an alternate Heather Rheims was again accusing an alternate—innocent—Eric Keric of unspeakable crimes. Or maybe she was embracing a confused but warm-hearted Janni.

Swallowing hard, she stepped away from the portal. Now she could hope for a reassignment, go exploring parallel universes for a more legitimate purpose, finding medical cures, scientific discoveries, even artistic works. Heather's vigilante streak made her a poor dispenser of justice. She would no longer solve crimes, not personal ones or political ones. The truth wasn't always clearcut, even in her own timeline.

Instead, she would remember Janni, keep the fond memories, maybe do some good things in her honor. She was alive, somewhere.

That was a truth Heather could hold on to.

THE BISTRO OF ALTERNATE REALITIES

The problem with closely parallel universes is that they all look the same. Sometimes, it takes an expert to notice the subtle differences, and only a professional timeline hunter can find variations for profitable exploitation by Alternitech Corp.

Heather Rheims arrived through the portal and took a deep, sweet breath to adjust herself to seemingly familiar surroundings. Among the myriad possible realities, the technology of Alternitech could fling her into nearby universes, worlds where decisions and alternatives had just slightly frayed the course of history. Thus, the city looked the same, the people were the same, most of the daily newspapers ran similar headlines … but some things were different. She just had to make her assessment.

Heather was the first one to reach the coffee shop. After wavering between possibilities, she chose a large table with eight chairs, which had always been sufficient for the doppelgangers who would show up. She picked a seat, then moved her pack to a different one, where she could see the door.

Leaving her equipment and her detailed archaeological notes on the table, she went to the coffee bar where the gaunt-looking young man with a wispy goatee—it was always a young man with a wispy goatee, no matter what universe she was in— and stared at the variety of hot and cold drinks, caffeinated and decaffeinated, sweet and bitter. Too many choices.

Though she came to the bistro on almost every journey through Alternitech's portals, she still had trouble making up her mind. Some people ordered the same hot beverage day after day, but Heather had never settled into a comfortable routine.

Unfortunately, that led to a crisis of decision every time she was faced with ordering coffee. After vacillating, she finally asked for a cappuccino with an extra shot of espresso, since she'd been feeling rundown. She took her wide cup back to the table and opened her thinscreen laptop so she could call up the esoteric archaeological details she was supposed to know by heart.

As a timeline hunter, Heather had been sent off into parallel universes in search of everything from medical breakthroughs to new music by the Beatles to conspiracy evidence in the JFK assassination. This time, she was a proxy archaeologist. She sipped her cappuccino and wiped foam off her lips before perusing the lengthy summaries of recent findings of ancient Greece and the Peloponnesian Wars.

Archaeology was not a rigorous science of trial and error and analysis: Finding artifacts that had been buried for untold centuries in uninhabited areas was primarily a matter of serendipity and luck. Some Turkish shepherd might go looking for part of his flock and discover a pile of ancient armor, the ruins of a fallen city, or documents sealed inside airtight containers. A single accidental find, like the Dead Sea Scrolls, might change the field forever—at least that was what the passionate young researcher Bruce Wanderlos had told Heather when he'd first hired her.

"Just because someone stumbled upon the ruins of ancient Troy in our timeline, doesn't mean the same accident happened in others." His eyes were bright, his pale brown hair curly and unkempt, but with a natural looseness that made the mess appear intentional and attractive. "And thus, the converse must also be true."

After receiving a large university grant Bruce had taken the controversial step of contracting Alternitech rather than going himself out into the field. Heather was assigned to go through the portal and look over current archaeology journals. "It's desk research, I know, and not terribly exciting—but if you copy the records of other digs, other discoveries that haven't been made yet in our universe, then I'll know exactly where to look here."

"Isn't that cheating?" Heather had asked.

He seemed so taken aback by her suggestion that she found him endearing. "This is acquiring information for science and history and the enrichment of mankind. It's not a game."

Now, in the coffee shop, she scrolled through items Bruce might be particularly interested in. The sophisticated software on her thinscreen allowed her to upload online records of any number of timeline-specific archaeological journals and scan for differences. The hardest part was deciding which place to go first. On one of her initial searches for Bruce, she had stopped at Mrs. Coffee Belgian Café and Bistro, intending just to have a cappuccino or a mocha while she planned her strategy—and then she'd discovered something incredibly alarming.

The door opened, and the tinkling silver bell announced the arrival of a new customer. She looked up to see, as expected, another Heather. She wondered which one this was and how many would be arriving for today's kaffeeklatsch. The other Heather, nearly identical except for her blouse, came over to drop her backpack in the chair beside Heather.

The barista blinked in surprise, as he always did, but by now most of the employees of Mrs. Coffee were used to the unusual event, convinced by the absurd explanation that all the Heathers were part of a Lookalike Club.

The new Heather went to the counter, swept her long cinnamon-brown hair out of her eyes and tucked it behind her shoulders. She decisively ordered a cappuccino, but without a shot of espresso. Heather wondered if maybe she should have done the same; did she really need the extra caffeine? She looked up to see another identical person step through the door. They would all be arriving soon.

Since, in her own world, Alternitech sent timeline hunters to parallel universes seeking to exploit differences, it only made sense that in many of those similar realities, other Alternitechs would send other timeline hunters, many of whom would be Heather's counterparts. The first time they'd stumbled upon each other was quite a shock, then a delight. Eventually Heather and her counterparts discovered that they could pool their resources.

Two more Heathers entered the coffee shop and bistro, standing in line to order their drinks, many of which were the same, though others had subtle variations, as was to be expected. Heather sat back and watched them all.

In the mix of universes, the people weren't always the same, but by now some of her doppelgangers were familiar to her. Most obvious was the Heather with a thin childhood scar on her cheek, a mark from when an abrupt gust of wind had blown a screen door into her face. Heather remembered that incident when she was a girl, but she had ducked aside and not been cut, as had most of her counterparts.

The first alternate Heather brought her cappuccino back to the table and sat down. Her opening question immediately identified her as Gloomy Heather. They all had quick nicknames, like the Seven Dwarves. "So are you dating anyone yet? I'm not. How's life in your timeline?"

Heather took another sip from her large cup to hide her embarrassment. "Not dating anyone at the moment, but it hasn't been that long."

"That archaeology guy's awfully cute," said another Heather, the one who had earned the nickname of Intense. "If my Sasha wasn't so damned good in bed, I'd ask Bruce out in a minute."

Intense Heather had hooked up with a fiery-eyed young rock musician, and the two had gone supernova with their initial romance. Intense rarely talked about anything else, and she had shown Sasha's picture to them all, in case they had a chance to bump into him in their own parallel universes. "Don't miss your chance. I almost did. Luckiest drink I ever spilled."

Intense had accidentally stumbled in a crowded bar on her way to a table of her own, spilling a glass of red wine on Sasha as he'd been heading for the door. He had responded with a flash of anger, and Intense Heather offered such abject apologies that the young musician burst into laughter and invited her to dinner. That had been the start.

So far, though, in every other parallel universe the Heathers had missed their chance, stumbling but catching the wine before it spilled, or losing Sasha before he walked out the door and never encountering him again. Heather had botched the opportunity entirely; when she mentally backtracked to the night in question, she realized that she had stayed home, unable to decide where to go.

Scar Heather sat down, picking up the conversation. "I'm flirting with Bruce, but I think he's just shy."

"Maybe I'll ask him out," said Gloomy, "but he'll probably say no."

"So what if he says no?" Intense responded. "You're not any worse off than if you don't ask at all. It's a no-brainer."

Heather found herself nodding. She had sensed the shy archaeologist's attraction for her, which he masked as appreciation for the successful work she'd done so far. Maybe she would push a little harder so that at least she'd have something to talk about with her counterparts the next time Intense bragged about her wild escapades with Sasha.

The smiling one who sat down was obviously Happily-Ever-After Heather, the one incarnation of all her parallel lives where circumstances had turned out perfect in every way. Two years before, most of the Heathers had been in a steady relationship with a computer programmer and part-time graphic designer named Perry. They'd fit together fairly well, but then Heather's sister Jamie had been killed, and the tragedy had torn her apart. Withdrawing, she'd taken out her resentment on Perry, and the two of them had parted.

But circumstances were slightly different in the universe of Happily-Ever-After Heather. Jamie had accidentally avoided becoming a random victim, and Happily-Ever-After had never faced the insurmountable stress in her relationship with Perry. Though they'd reached a crisis of personal goals and feelings, they had decided to work out their differences, investing in their bond instead of drawing apart. Perry and Happily-Ever-After had gotten married a year later, and now they had a fine home, both had good careers, and everything was perfect. The other Heathers halfway resented their counterpart, but most of all they envied her.…

When finally all of the alternate Heathers had their coffees and sat down at the table, Intense Heather unzipped her pack and withdrew her thinscreen. "Time to get down to business. The portals will be back before you know it." All eight of them looked at their watches with comical simultaneity.

Each Heather took out her carefully culled and organized database of archaeological information from her own universe. Instead of spending hours sifting through library records or digging out obscure references in journals, all the Heathers sat down for coffee and conversation. That way they could simply exchange all the files they had collated from their homes. In an hour of swapping and comparing records, the eight Heathers could achieve as many discoveries as if they had gone on eight separate timeline hunts.

This cooperative efficiency had made her quite a success in all her incarnations—at least all of the ones who showed up at the coffee shop. Heather's counterparts and their identical goals yielded a synergy that allowed each of them to deliver clue after clue to the endearingly appreciative Bruce Wanderlos. Most of the differences turned out to be of no interest to anyone, but occasionally they hit the jackpot.

And while their thinscreens were humming and exchanging, compiling and rejecting, Heather had a chance to listen to advice from her alternate selves. It was like having a sounding board better than a best friend, drawing upon common experience and shared hearts. The Heathers who had made bad decisions did their best to help those who had not yet encountered the risky situation.

At first, Heather had been somewhat hurt to discover that they'd labeled her Indecisive Heather, but the reasons were obvious even to herself and she couldn't fault them for it. She had come to depend on these conversations and personal strategy sessions. She rarely made up her own mind anymore, but hesitated too often, losing opportunities.

"I've got an idea," said Intense, slurping her double espresso. She targeted Gloomy. "You always say you missed your chance, that by sheer bad luck you're never in the right place at the right time. Believe me, half of it's your own problem because you don't take any chances—but here I'm offering you one. Switch with me. Go home to my universe and spend a day or two with Sasha."

Gloomy's eyes widened. "I couldn't do that. He's your—"

"And you think he'd be cheating on me if he slept with you? You are me. God, if I was the one who hadn't been laid in two years, I'd sure hope one of you might take pity on me."

"But … but how will I ever fool him? We don't have the same history. We look the same, but your personality's entirely—"

"You wouldn't have to fool him, Heather dear. He knows what I do for a living. In fact, he'd get a kick out of it, and you'd give me a rest. Frankly, I'm a bit sore, and I could do with a day or two of just sitting at home and reading a book. You've probably got the same unread novels on your shelf that I do."

The other Heathers immediately went into a detailed discussion about the morality and wisdom of this plan. Heather suspected many of them were secretly hoping for their own chance with Sasha.

Happily-Ever-After looked deeply uncomfortable. "Your lives are what you made them, every mistake, every decision. Why can't you be satisfied with the way things are? It's nice to compare notes with each other, but this is drastic."

"Sure," said Scar. "Listen to advice from the one who has a perfect life." Happily-Ever-After blushed as if ashamed of her own good fortune.

When all their databases had been exchanged, they finished their coffees and picked up the dishes. Heather was glad she didn't have to make the choice that Gloomy Heather faced. It would have taken her a month to make up her mind.

"All right," said Gloomy, "if I don't do this, you'll never let me complain again." She forced a wan smile. "I'll go back through your portal, you go back through mine." Gloomy and Intense shook hands like businessmen, then realized how absurd they looked and gave each other a simultaneous hug.

"Be careful, Sasha just might burn you out," Intense said.

"That'll be … quite a new experience for me," Gloomy answered.

They all split up. Heather shouldered her backpack and went to her own rendezvous point, where the discreet portal would shimmer through the air.

They would all meet again at another bistro in another parallel universe.

●　○　●

When she delivered her results to the technicians at Alternitech, Bruce Wanderlos was there waiting with a shy smile. While he skimmed the results, she went to the locker room to shower and change, getting back into decent clothes instead of the plain "don't notice me" outfit Alternitech asked its timeline hunters to wear.

Before she left for the day, though, the archaeologist met her outside the dressing room door.

His eyes were shining, his face flushed, and he took a quick step toward her as if he wanted to give her a happy kiss. "You don't realize what you found there! There's a fleet of Greek warships sunk in a bay off the Anatolian Peninsula. They've been preserved in the deep, cold water. According to these papers, one of the archaeologists believes it was Agamemnon's fleet in the Trojan War!"

Heather recognized that such a discovery would make a name for Bruce. "Sounds like you've got your work cut out for you."

Bruce shook his head and drew a deep breath. "I don't know how I can ever thank you. I just wish—"

Impulsively, remembering her Intense and Happily-Ever-After counterparts, she said quickly before she could think about it too much, "Well, you could ask me out for a drink—or dinner, if you feel really grateful."

He seemed taken aback. "I didn't know that—I didn't think ... are you sure it's all right if we mix business and socialization?"

Heather raised her eyebrows. "Bruce, if this is as big a discovery as you say, you won't need to hire my services any more."

"All right." He was delighted at his doubly unexpected good fortune.

She gave him her number and address, and they arranged a time. "Oh, and Bruce?" Heather called, giddy at her own good luck. "If this discovery is so significant, you better find someplace that doesn't just serve hamburgers."

"I … I'll make reservations."

●　○　●

"Just because a seafood chain has the word 'lobster' in its name doesn't mean it's a fancy restaurant," said Scar, but she looked more amused than disappointed.

Heather sat back and drank from her double mocha. "Well, I don't care. It was the nicest evening I've had in a long time."

"He took me to an Italian restaurant," said Silly Heather, who always had trouble opening up her real feelings and covered it all with a joke, even among her identical counterparts.

Happily-Ever-After just grinned. "I'm so pleased you finally made the decision to do it. Part of me wishes you'd try to patch things up with Perry, though, because we're so happy together."

"We know," groaned Intense.

"Perry's married again in my universe," said Heather. "I took too long—"

"He's only engaged in mine," said Scar.

Quiet Heather watched them all; she was one of the few who hadn't gotten up the nerve to nudge

Bruce into a date, but she looked as if she might change her mind.

Intense seemed inordinately edgy and disturbed. All the doppelgangers were curious to hear the story of Gloomy's "perfectly licit" affair with the passionate Sasha … but Gloomy hadn't joined them today, or the previous two meetings.

"I'm sure it turned out all right," Heather said, sensing how deeply disturbed her normally gruff counterpart was.

"She probably just wants him for a few more days to get her fill," Scar suggested.

"Sasha can sometimes be a little … intense."

"You're a perfect match for him then," Silly said. Some of the other Heathers chuckled, but the Intense one did not.

"Bruce asked me out again," Heather announced, "on his own initiative this time."

"How long do you think I should wait until I sleep with him?" said another one.

"Are you kidding? He could barely manage a goodnight kiss."

"He's shy, not celibate," said Scar.

"Did you ask about his family?"

"Did you tell him about Jamie?"

"He seemed very sad to hear it when I did."

"How serious is he about all this?"

"How serious am I about this? It's too soon to ask those questions."

"He's never been married, has he?"

"No. I asked him point blank."

"I wish he wouldn't hold his fork like that. Nobody ever taught him table manners."

"We had pizza, so I didn't get a chance to notice."

"Who cares about his table manners? It's his personality that counts, and Bruce is very nice."

Heather listened to the rapid-fire exchange of alternative dates that she could have had. It seemed as if she got to know Bruce Wanderlos better by hearing all the comparisons ... but it was unfair. Did she really need all of these surrogate Heathers to live her life for her?

"You're all pathetic," said Intense. "Just listen to yourselves! I was always fairly strong and independent—and so are all of you. But now you sound like a bunch of airhead cheerleaders in a locker room."

"Excuse me," said Happily-Ever-After, "but you were insufferable yourself when you started seeing Sasha. I don't think I'm the only one who was tired of hearing about all your sex."

"Maybe you're just upset to be away from him," said Quiet Heather.

"Or maybe you're jealous because another one of us is with him," said Scar, "despite all of your assertions to the contrary."

Someone else came in to the bistro, and Intense looked up quickly, hoping that she would see her Gloomy counterpart return, but it was just a middle-aged man looking for a sandwich. Angry and frustrated, Intense grabbed her pack and took her thinscreen, though she hadn't finished exchanging files with all of her doppelgangers. She stormed out of the coffee shop while the other Heathers looked after her.

"Something's worse than she's admitting," said Heather. "Most of us would be worried in that situation, but not go ballistic."

Scar finished her coffee while Happily-Ever-After gathered their cups. "We still haven't settled how fast should we push this with Bruce. How far do we go?"

"We'll each have to decide that for ourselves," said Heather.

All of the others looked at her in surprise as if she had just told a joke.

●　○　●

On their second date Heather and Bruce went out to a foreign film with subtitles that Heather thought was supposed to impress her, though neither of them much enjoyed—or understood—the movie.

Following the lead of what some of her counterparts had done, she decided to tell him about her sister Jamie, showed him pictures. As she expected, Bruce was very understanding and compassionate without being maudlin.

Still, she felt odd every moment, a strange sense of déjà vu—as if she were stuck in an old rerun of "It's a Wonderful Life." Some people would have considered it an advantage to test out choices and decisions, then rewind and try again if they didn't work. Would Bruce himself think it was cheating, in a completely different sense from how he used someone else's archaeology work?

In an awkward yet sweet way, he asked her to come to his apartment for coffee—she was getting tired of coffee, but she listened to his words, which he had obviously rehearsed in front of a mirror. She ended up staying for three hours, but the whole time they just sat on the sofa and talked. He didn't even try to kiss her until she was about to leave. Heather supposed that the next time she met her counterparts in the coffee shop, her doppelgangers would be full of alternate endings for this evening, some of them lurid, some of them embarrassing. But she liked the way her own had turned out, with or without coaching from her other selves....

Thanks to Heather's results, Bruce now had more archaeological work than he could handle for years.

Alternitech timeline hunters were expensive, and his grant money had nearly run out, so he finished his request for Heather's services, though he intended to keep seeing her on a more personal level.

On her last outing for the project, Heather went tentatively back to Mrs. Coffee, not sure if she even wanted to keep discussing their budding relationship with the other Heathers. Part of the excitement of romance was the spontaneity, the unpredictability, and she had an unfair advantage if she already knew a dozen possible ways that any evening might turn out.

Intense Heather's boyfriend Sasha seemed too unpredictable, a loose cannon with mood swings and fiery passion, while her own former relationship with Perry had been too sedate and comfortable. She didn't know how it was going to turn out with Bruce … and she wasn't sure she wanted to know. This wasn't being indecisive, as was her too-common flaw—it was being accepting.

Though the archaeology project was over, the Heathers would continue to meet in the coffee shop, discussing ways to increase their discoveries in alternate timelines. But Heather wasn't sure she was interested in talking about her personal life. Maybe she wanted to make her own choices for a change.

Today she was one of the last to arrive. Inside, it looked as if Intense was having a nervous breakdown.

She shouted, "You don't understand! I'm terrified for her. I got her into this! I egged her into making her decision—and what if Sasha's hurt her?"

"He wouldn't hurt her," said one of the other Heathers, trying to be soothing.

"Oh, and you're the expert on his unstable personality? He's got problems. He flies into rages. He's supposed to take medication, but all the time the asshole convinces himself he doesn't need it."

"That doesn't sound like the man you've been talking about all along," said Scar.

Intense wrung her hands. "He's not like that usually. He can be sweet and romantic and passionate—but other times he just flies off the handle. I could sense he was getting impatient with me, said I was too domineering, that I was like a bulldozer. I thought maybe he'd want someone a bit more passive. I thought he'd like her. But sometimes being passive just provokes the abusive streak in him. What if he's killed her? My God!"

"You're overreacting, Heather."

"Am I? It's been five times, and she hasn't come back. And you know that I can't return to my own universe unless she comes through and opens the portal. There has to be an exchange. I can't just go get her."

"It was a decision that she made," Heather said, standing beside the crowded table.

Looking alarmed at the discord among the identical women, the goateed barista stood close to the phone as if contemplating a call to 9-1-1.

Heather continued, looking at her counterparts. "You made up your mind. She made up her mind. We've all made up our minds—but we spend endless hours in here talking and discussing and gossiping. Dammit, my whole life has become a committee!"

"But what am I supposed to do about … her?" Intense said. She seemed to know something much more dangerous about Sasha than she had ever revealed them, especially Gloomy.

"Do whatever you decide, and then you'll have to live with it."

Seeing the group of Heathers in the coffee shop, she wondered how many other counterparts had already left the kaffeeklatsch, not wanting to hear about other lives or experience regrets for incorrect decisions. Of all the infinite universes, maybe only this handful of Heathers felt the need to commiserate with each other, share secrets and depend upon someone else.

She didn't even bother to remove her backpack. "I'd better be off doing my work. This isn't … what I want anymore. It's my life, after all, and I feel like I'm in a room full of dress rehearsals."

"Don't you want to wait and find out if the other Heather comes back?" said Intense. "Maybe she's all right, or maybe Sasha just kept her for an extra while."

"You know, I've decided it isn't relevant to me," she answered. "Because there are probably timelines where it happens every possible way. I need to focus on my life as a participant, not a spectator."

"Wait, you'll want to hear about what happened with Bruce last night," said Scar, raising her eyebrows. Several of the others leaned forward, eager as predators.

"What happened on your own date?" someone asked her before she could leave. "Weren't you supposed to go out with him again, too?"

But Heather turned away. "I'll just keep it to myself, for good or bad. Why should I live vicariously through all of you, when I can do it myself first-hand?"

From the set of troubled looks on their faces, Heather realized she had struck a nerve, that the thoughts had crossed most of their minds already. "Good luck," she said to herself and to all of them, then left the coffee shop behind.

Rough Draft

with Rebecca Moesta

After a decade during which he wrote and published nothing new, the fan letters dwindled to a few a year.

"Dear Mr. Coren, You're the best science fiction writer ever!"

"Dear Mr. Coren, Your book *Divergent Lines* changed my life. I felt as if you were speaking directly to me, and you helped me work through some major issues."

The entire experience, though great for the ego, had ultimately proved meaningless. Eventually he'd been forced to return the money for the second book advance, because he simply couldn't do it again. After enjoying a pleasant day in the sun, Mitchell Coren had retreated to his small apartment to live a normal life. The gleaming Nebula Award and the silver Hugo—both dusty now—were little more than knickknacks on the mantle of a fireplace that he never used.

Having convinced himself of the wisdom of J.D. Salinger's approach to authorial fame, Mitchell had squelched all thoughts of returning to writing. He immersed himself in a normal life with all its petty concerns.

Today, with an indifference born of long practice, Mitchell opened his bills and junk mail before finally tearing open the padded envelope that obviously contained a book. Another intrusion, no doubt. An annoying reminder of his old life. He still received advance reading copies from editors trying to wheedle a rare cover quote from him, rough draft manuscripts from aspiring authors who begged for comments or critiques, and books presented to him by new authors who had been inspired by his lone published novel.

Inside this envelope, however, he found his own name on the dust jacket of a novel he had never written.

INFERNITIES

Mitchell Coren

Multiple Award-winning Author of *Divergent Lines*

Whirling flakes of confusion compacted into a hard snowball in the pit of his stomach. "What the hell?"

His initial, and obvious, thought was that someone had stolen his name. But that didn't make sense. Though many editorial positions had changed in the decade since he'd published *Divergent Lines*, Mitchell was still well enough known in the insular science fiction community that somebody in the field would have noticed an imposter. Besides, how much could his byline be worth after all this time? It wasn't worth stealing.

Someone had tucked a folded sheet of paper between the book's front cover and the endpaper. He read it warily.

Dear Mr. Coren,

As a longtime fan of yours, I thought you'd appreciate seeing this novel I came across in a parallel universe.

I'm a timeline hunter by profession. Perhaps you've heard of Alternitech? Our company uses a proprietary technology to open gateways into alternate realities. My colleagues and I explore these parallel universes for breakthroughs or useful discrepancies that Alternitech can profitably exploit: medical and scientific advances, historical discoveries, artistic variations. My specialty is the creative arts.

I stumbled upon this book in an alternate timeline while searching for a new Mario Puzo. Since the science fiction market isn't nearly as large or profitable as the mainstream, I couldn't spend much time checking out its background, but a brief search showed that the 'alternate' Mitchell Coren published a dozen or so short stories after Divergent Lines, then produced this second novel. I'm hoping Alternitech will want to arrange for its publication, but naturally I felt you should see it first.

With deepest respect,

Jeremy Cardiff

Mitchell stared at the letter with mistrust and growing irritation. He had heard of this company that searched alternate realities for everything from new Beatles records, to evidence of UFOs or Kennedy assassination conspiracies, to cures for obscure diseases. He could understand the more humanitarian objectives, but why fiction? What gave Alternitech the right to infringe on his life like this?

He opened to the dust jacket photo and saw that the picture did resemble him, though this other Mitchell Coren wore a different hairstyle and a cocky, self-assured grin. The bio mentioned that after completing *Infernities* he was "already at work on his next novel."

Oddly unsettled, Mitchell pushed the book away. Its very existence raised too many disturbing questions.

•　○　•

Three increasingly urgent phone calls to his former agent went unreturned. Since Mitchell had neither delivered anything new nor generated much income, his agent wasn't in a great hurry to attend to his so-called emergency. Even in the days when he'd briefly been a hot client, Mitchell had been relatively high-maintenance, needing encouragement and constant contact.

He decided to contact his entertainment attorney instead. After all, Sheldon Freiburg charged by the hour and therefore had an incentive to get right on the matter.

"Mitch Coren! I haven't heard from you since the last ice age." Freiburg's voice was bluff and hearty on the telephone. "What on earth have you been doing? You dropped off the map."

"I've been working a real-world job, Sheldon. You know, regular paycheck, benefits … security?"

"Yeah, I've heard of those. Hopped off the old fame-and-fortune bandwagon, eh?"

"A modicum of fame, not a whole lot of fortune—as you well know."

Freiburg had handled the entertainment contracts for the two movie options on *Divergent Lines.* Mitchell had been young and naïve then, believing the Hollywood hype and enthusiasm. He'd been surrounded by smiling fast-talkers whose eager assertions of certain box-office appeal and guaranteed studio support were built on a foundation as strong as a soap bubble. After the attorney's fees and the agent's commission, the option money had been just enough to pay off his car, which was now ten years old.

"So, Mitchell," Freiburg said now, "people don't call me unless they have a situation—either good or bad—so let's hear it."

"Someone's trying to publish an unauthorized Mitchell Coren novel."

"You've actually done other work?" The lawyer sounded surprised. "Something new? I thought you'd turned hermit on us. Did somebody steal your manuscript?"

"This is trickier than that. It isn't exactly a matter of stealing. This is a novel from a parallel universe, and Alternitech wants to get it published here." He explained the situation in full.

"Oh, that is tricky—but not unheard of. Listen, since it's Tuesday, I'll give you a special deal, a quick and inexpensive answer."

"Inexpensive? You've changed in the last ten years, Sheldon."

The lawyer chuckled. "How could I help it? The whole world has changed. But you're not going to like what I have to say."

Mitchell braced himself, clutching the receiver; thankfully, Freiburg could not see his tense expression.

"Precedents have been set in this area. In every dispute about the use of materials from alternate universes, Alternitech has come out the winner. I'm convinced the company spends as much money each year on their team of lawyers as they did developing their parallel universe gateway. You'd be wasting your money to try and block the publication. Compared to the rest of the entertainment industry, authors and books are minnows in an ocean. Even the Big Fish in the music and film industries haven't won a single case.

"Alternitech's timeline hunters bring back intellectual property that might conceivably belong to a counterpart in this universe. The first big case was when one of their music specialists, a guy named Jeremy Cardiff—"

"That's who sent me the novel."

"Great," Freiburg said, then continued, ignoring the interruption. "In Alternitech v the Carpenter Estate, Cardiff found several new albums by the Carpenters, in an alternate reality where Karen Carpenter never died of anorexia. The CDs sounded like the same old shit to me, but don't underestimate the huge amount of money generated by piped-in background music. The Carpenter Estate sued, citing copyright infringement and unlawful exploitation of a creative work.

"Alternitech countered that since Karen Carpenter was dead in this universe, she could not 'create' new works after the date of her death. They also argued using an old favorite of the pharmaceutical companies, that since Alternitech had made such a substantial investment developing their technology, they deserved to reap the benefits of its commercial exploitation.

"The ruling sided with the Carpenter Estate insofar as establishing a 'fair percentage' of profits that should go to the creator's counterpart in this reality—fifteen percent, I think it was. But since Alternitech's timeline hunters did all the work obtain the property, kind of like salvage hunters on the high seas, they were granted full control of its use. Similar lawsuits have been raised by individual movie producers, screenwriters, directors, and even actors who resent the release of 'new films' starring them for which they never got paid. Like I said, in every case, they lose."

Mitchell remembered that one of the alternate Mel Gibson films had caused something of a stir, because the parallel-universe version of the actor had received an Academy Award for a role that this timeline's Gibson had turned down.

Freiburg continued. "When you get right down to it, Mitch, record companies and movie studios don't want the individual artists to win. Alternitech provides them with completely finished new work for a fraction of the cost or effort of making it themselves. Much less hassle, too. They just distribute the work through their normal channels and pay a standard percentage of artist's royalties directly to Alternitech. Then, if and only if the court orders it, Alternitech cuts a teeny weeny check to our own world's parallel artist or company or estate, and everyone is happy. Well, almost everyone."

"So you're saying I shouldn't even try, Sheldon? It's not … not right!"

"Mitch, if Paul McCartney can't win, then a mere sci-fi novelist doesn't stand a snowball's chance." He paused as if reconsidering. "On the other hand, Mitch my friend, I just thought of a factor that's ironically in your favor, if you really want to stop publication. There's a very real chance that Alternitech won't even bother with your little book. Look at your royalty statements. You're a science fiction writer ten years out of the public eye. Oh sure, there'd be a limited audience for a 'lost unpublished work' by Mitchell Coren … but it isn't exactly a Margaret Mitchell sequel to Gone with the Wind. If this Cardiff guy is a fan of yours, contact him and tell him how you feel. Who knows, he might do you a favor and pretend he never found it."

Mitchell didn't know whether to feel stung or take heart from the possibility.

●　○　●

Distracted and fretting, he polished the two awards on his mantel—something he hadn't done for the better part of a year. They looked quite impressive, he had to admit, and certainly gave him bragging rights. His occasional visitors asked about them, and he answered with feigned modesty. The awards seemed so irrelevant to his current life.

These days, Mitchell used his skills as a wordsmith in the unglamorous but stable profession of technical writing, producing essential documentation and annual reports for a manufacturing firm. Although it was a challenge to write compelling prose about new cereal box designs or recyclable plastic bottles, he was a master at slanting his text toward investors or consumers or environmental agencies, as needed.

Many of his coworkers—what the science fiction world called "mundanes"—were aspiring writers who never managed to finish or submit stories. Few of them knew about his past, however, since Mitchell rarely mentioned his novel.

As he rubbed a fingerprint off the Nebula's clear Lucite surface, looking at the suspended bits of metal shavings and semi-precious stones that formed a sparkling galaxy, he thought back to those brief, heady days. They were just memories now, but he wouldn't trade them for anything.

Divergent Lines had appeared with a splash like a giant water balloon. An excerpt of the novel had been published in Analog as the cover story and won that month's readers' poll. The novel itself had generated rave reviews and was immediately dubbed "a new classic" by critics and his fellow SF authors.

He had been welcomed as a hero at the World Science Fiction Convention. He'd always read science fiction, but had never attended a con before. The fans surprised him at panels, listening to everything he said. They lined up for his book signings in the autograph hall or followed him and asked embarrassingly earnest questions about details he himself had never considered.

When Mitchell went to the Hugo Awards ceremony, he found himself plunged into a sea of unreality as the emcee announced his name as the winner. Astonished and grinning, he stumbled up to the podium and held up his silver rocket ship with mixed feelings of shock and giddy triumph.

The following spring, thanks to the continued buzz, *Divergent Lines* had been a shoe-in for the final Nebula ballot. New to the entire experience, Mitchell stood like a lost puppy in the lobby and the bar, surrounded by luminaries of the genre. He recognized their names from the covers of well-loved books, famous writers ranging from Grand Masters to prolific hacks, all of them legendary and, for the most part, personable.

He'd been in a daze. These Titans of science fiction talked to him as a peer, praised his novel. Mithcell found it unnerving, and he began to wonder how he could ever live up to their expectations. Did he deserve so much praise and success? What if his next work didn't measure up to their expectations? Would he be exposed as a fraud and cast out of this distinguished circle of authors? How would he bear the humiliation?

His publisher paid for his Nebula banquet ticket, and Mitchell was treated as a celebrity at their table.

With his stomach tied in knots, he could summon no appetite at all. In an agony of anticipation, he endured the drawn-out meal, the mandatory chit-chat, the interminable banquet speaker. By the time the awards finally began, plodding through each category as if in a calculated effort to increase his anxiety, Mitchell had convinced himself that he had no chance of winning. He was a newcomer. He had no track record. He had never played the politics of exchanging recommendations. He had not campaigned for the award. These writers couldn't possibly consider him a friend and certainly didn't owe him any favors.

And yet the name in the presenter's envelope said *Divergent Lines*. The Nebula seemed even more amazing than the Hugo, because this honor came from his peers, fellow professionals who supposedly knew good writing when they saw it. As Mitchell stood clutching the award, he imagined that someday, when he stood at the Pearly Gates and looked back on his entire life, this would be the high point....

After that night, though, Mitchell Coren never wrote another word of fiction. He had left the science fiction community behind and let *Divergent Lines* stand as his sole legacy.

●　○　●

Even in his heyday, Mitchell had not spent much time with die-hard science fiction fans. Not because he didn't like them—he appreciated anyone who bought and loved his novel. But he didn't understand their intensity or their passions and usually ended up feeling outclassed when they wanted to talk shop.

He met Jeremy Cardiff at a quiet place called Mrs. Coffee, a small bistro with shaded outside tables where they could have a conversation in a pleasant atmosphere. Mitchell didn't know which of them was more nervous. He could see in the timeline hunter's eyes that Jeremy was a bona fide Fan.

"This is really an honor, Mr. Coren. I've always been an admirer of *Divergent Lines*, and now that I've read *Infernities*, there's no doubt in my mind that you're one of my all-time favorite authors. I felt so surprised and fortunate to have found the book." Jeremy, a youngish man with a thin face, long hair, and a neatly-trimmed brown beard, looked like a waif hoping for a pat on the head. His blue eyes were wide, his smile tentative.

Mitchell took a drink of coffee, then cleared his throat. "Well, Mr. Cardiff, that's what I'm here to talk to you about."

"Please, call me Jeremy." Then the younger man's face fell as he interpreted Mitchell's reluctant tone.

Mitchell chose his words as carefully as he would have in preparing a viewgraph presentation for the board of the manufacturing company. He wasn't sure his reasons would make sense to anyone but himself. Though he knew he didn't exactly have a legal case, he might be able to play the celebrity card. Perhaps by asking a special favor from his number one fan, he could get what he needed. "I think you're perceptive enough to understand why I don't want the novel published here. It's not my book. Somebody else wrote it."

"No, Mr. Coren. You wrote it. Another version of you, maybe, but it was still your talent, your creativity. When I was in college I read and reread *Divergent Lines* until my copy fell apart, and I've been waiting ten years for a new novel by the same author. When I found *Infernities*, I sent you the physical book I brought back through the portal, but I made a photocopy. I'm already on my second time through it. It's brilliant—full of intricate layers and nuances."

Mitchell desperately wanted to ask which book he thought was better. Dedicated readers like Jeremy were generally his toughest customers and his harshest critics and, because Mitchell didn't think a new novel could ever live up to their expectations, he had decided not to try.

"That man may have the same name and the same genetics as I do, but he grew up in a parallel universe with a different set of circumstances. He's not me. He obviously reached a different decision about his career. But I didn't write *Infernities*, and if you published it here in our universe, people would see it as my own work, no matter how many disclaimers you put on it."

"But it's good, sir. Have you read it?"

"No, I don't dare. It would seem almost … plagiaristic."

As if clinging to hope, Jeremy said, "So … are you writing something of your own? Maybe a book that's similar to *Infernities*?"

"No. I'm not writing anything."

The young man looked at his coffee as if it were poison. He didn't seem angry at Mitchell's attitude, just deeply disappointed. "Then I don't understand. What made you stop writing? I mean, you got the royal treatment. People were lined up waiting for your next book. You had a contract to fulfill, didn't you?"

"Yes. And I … decided to return the advance."

"But why? It just doesn't make sense."

"Why? I'd already won the highest accolades in my field." Mitchell spoke softly, but his voice grew more intense. "Whether through brilliance or sheer dumb luck I muddled my way to the pinnacle of success my first time out of the starting gate. *Divergent Lines* was hailed as the best book of the year, won all the awards, got spectacular reviews in every periodical from *Publishers Weekly* and *Kirkus* to *Locus* and *Chronicle. Library Journal* called it an instant classic."

Mitchell sighed. "Don't you see? The weight of it all gets oppressive. Where could I possibly go from there? There's no place but down." An edge of bitterness sharpened his tone. "It's a very long way down. No matter how good it was, my second book—*Infernities* or whatever I might've called it—would never be good enough. The fans and the critics certainly aren't kind unless your sophomore effort is unbelievably spectacular.

"As it stands right now, I'll go down in history as the author of a great novel. But if I published twenty other books, regardless of how well-written they might be, I can tell you some of the review quotes already: 'A solid novel, but not as inspired as *Divergent Lines.*' Or 'A fine effort, though it doesn't live up to the promise of its predecessor.' Or, worse yet, 'A disappointing follow-on to the author's first novel.' "

Jeremy frowned at what Mitchell was saying. "I think you're too hard on your fans, sir. We would have followed you. Even after ten years, most of us still want to read whatever you have to say."

"Maybe I don't have anything else to say," Mitchell said. "I can name author after author who falls into that category. Being successful is a Catch-22. If your first novel is a smash hit, an award winner and a critical success, it might mean your career has momentum and you're launched. On the other hand, it could mean your writing will never be good enough again. What should I have done—expanded *Divergent Lines* and written a couple of unnecessary sequels, so I could call it a trilogy? I could have licensed my universe, farmed it out to other authors, but that just didn't seem right to me. Either way, I would have been crucified by the fans and the critics."

"Just by the snobs," Jeremy said, "not by the fans. But you disappeared from fandom altogether. When's the last time you went to a science fiction convention?"

"The WorldCon where I got my Hugo was the first and last. I stopped reading *Locus* and *Chronicle* and *Ansible* after one of them ran an editorial about one-hit wonders that led off with 'What ever happened to Mitchell Coren?'" He looked at his coffee. "I didn't stand a chance of keeping up the momentum in my career. Fans and critics are too unpredictable. So I controlled the only part of the equation that I could control: I stopped writing fiction. My life is stable now that I've accepted the wisdom of anonymity. But if Alternitech publishes this apocryphal second novel that I didn't really write, then I'll be at the mercy of the public's expectations again. Please, don't do it."

Disappointment and resignation filled Jeremy's eyes as he unzipped his backpack and reached inside to withdraw a thick stack of photocopied pages. "Look, this is my only copy. What happens to it is not really supposed to be my decision. Alternitech owns proprietary rights to whatever I bring back through parallel universes. Still, no matter how much I loved this novel, I have to admit that this doesn't have the equivalent value to Alternitech of, say, an unknown collection of Sherlock Holmes stories by Arthur Conan Doyle or the Dean Koontz/Stephen King collaboration I uncovered once. I think people deserve to read it. I was going to have you autograph this for me." Jeremy slid the stack of papers across the table. "But now I guess you'd better keep it, so you'll know there aren't any other copies in existence. You decide what to do. It's your call, Mr. Coren. It's your book."

"I—" Mitchell started to speak, but found his voice choked with emotion. He took a long drink of his now-tepid coffee and started again. "Well … don't you want to keep it? You said you were reading it."

Jeremy shook his head. "If you know I have a copy, you'd always worry that someday I'd be tempted to post it on the Internet. It's better if you keep it."

The papers felt warm in Mitchell's hands. His vision blurred, and he took a moment to compose himself. "I … didn't expect this."

"I'm a musician myself, Mr. Coren. I write and record songs, but I haven't had much success so far.

It was a minor consolation when I found that I did have a hit record in an alternate universe, but nothing here yet. I was the one who brought back the new music for that whole Karen Carpenter debacle, and I don't feel very good about it. As a musician, I thought Carpenter or her estate should have had some control over her own creative work, no matter which incarnation made the album. The same goes for you, sir. If you're uncomfortable about having *Infernities* published, then …" He shrugged.

"I can't tell you how much this means to me."

"I think I understand." Jeremy slurped his decaf cappuccino. "Besides, I'm your fan. I can't think of anything cooler than to know I am the only person in this entire universe who's read your new novel."

• O •

Dozens of the loose photocopy sheets wadded up under the fireplace grate made for good kindling. Mitchell rolled the remaining loose pages of twenty-pound bond into plump literary logs, rubber-banded them, and set them on the log holder above the crumpled pages. Then he fanned out the hardcover book and flattened it across the white paper logs. He stood back to observe the diminutive funeral pyre with a sense of uneasiness.

He should have felt relieved.

This potential source of humiliation or disruption would soon be dealt with. The book would no longer be in his life, could no longer irritate or goad him by its very existence. No fans would have a chance to either criticize or clamor for more. The chapter would be closed.

Yes, Mitchell was definitely relieved.

After he lit the match, he hesitated for a long, indecisive moment before finally touching the flame to the edge of one of the loose sheets. There. A burnt offering to a cruel muse.

As the fire caught, guilt gnawed at the ragged edges of his mind. There was something intrinsically criminal about burning a book, especially the only copies of a book. While this event would not go down in history with the sacking of the Library of Alexandria, it was still a loss to at least some tiny backwater of the literary sea—especially to the hopeful fans who had waited so long for any work by Mitchell Coren.

The flames grew higher, devouring the loose pages and curling the glossy dust jacket of *Infernities*. An interesting play on words, he thought. Infinity, Alternative, and Eternity all rolled together. Now he could add "Inferno" to the quadruple entendre. He wondered how it related to the story.

Didn't he owe it to himself at least to read his own work, to see what he could have done with his talent? *Infernities* was tangible proof that in some other reality his author-self had overcome the pressure and the expectations. But how? Didn't that mean that he, too, could do it?

No. He'd made the right decision. He thought with some satisfaction of the author photo blackening and blistering, cremating his cocksure successful doppelganger. The man had dared to risk his reputation, his spotless literary legacy, to write this second novel and offer it to an unpredictable reading public. He had dared. Had risked …

With a groan of annoyance and frustration Mitchell snatched the hardcover from the fire, dropped it to the floor, and stamped on it to put out the flames at the edges. He bent and picked up the singed novel that had disrupted his calm life.

As he picked up the blackened book, Mitchell's lips flickered in a smile. Though he still had no intention of publishing the novel, he would hold onto the book as a goad. Just to keep him honest. To remind himself of what could be.

He had his own ideas for new stories and novels, of course. Every writer did. The ideas had never stopped coming, and he had jotted down notes during lunch hours at his tech-writing job. Some of the outlines were damn good, but he had been too afraid of failure to write the books, believing it better to let readers live with his mysterious seclusion than to risk them shaking their heads in disappointment.

Yet his alternate self had somehow shaken off the fear of failure. Therefore, it could be done. And that sincere, appreciative look he had seen in Jeremy Cardiff's eyes told Mitchell he still had an audience, no matter how small....

Some authors were motivated to write strictly for the critics, for the kudos and awards. Others wanted the money and name recognition of sales, with big print runs and splashy publicity. Some wrote only for themselves, giving the finger to anyone else's expectations. But why had he become a writer?

Now there was a group to whom he owed something: his fans—the readers who understood what he was trying to do and who saw him as a human being with a talent that should not simply be thrown away. Those fans would enjoy whatever he wrote.

Certainly, a few of them went to the crazy fringe, seeing him as a guru with unparalleled insight into their particular problems. But most were just regular people. If he struck the right note, his pool of fans would be large; if he chose a path that was too esoteric, the numbers might dwindle. In either case, the readers still deserved his respect.

Mitchell looked at the charred copy of *Infernities* he held. He realized now that burning the novel was selfish. There were thousands (or maybe only dozens) of people like Jeremy Cardiff, who would have enjoyed this book if he allowed it to be published.

Setting the burned hardcover down, he opened the bottom file drawer of his desk where he kept the folder of notes and ideas that were just too good to throw away. If he was going to bury this cuckoo's egg of a book, then he was obligated to give the readers something in exchange.

Mitchell skimmed his outlines. He had forgotten how clever or thought-provoking many of them were. Had he intended to be an Emily Dickinson, locking his notes away in a box for someone else to find after he died? Not long ago, he had been tempted to burn these, too.

Now he would write some of them.

As he flipped through his notes, the ideas reached a critical mass, and Mitchell saw how he could combine concepts and characters. What might have been simple short story ideas now became enough material for a multi-layered novel. It wouldn't be just like *Divergent Lines*, but so what? It would still be good, still be worth writing.

He spread the papers out on his desk. He had an old, outdated laptop computer and plenty of time during his lunch hours. Some of the greatest works of literature had been completed a few pages at a time during lunch breaks....

Mitchell glanced at the fireplace, where the fire had now died to a pile of orange embers. The photocopied novel was now nothing but ash.

On the mantel above, his Hugo and Nebula awards reflected the dull glow. He turned away from them and focused on his desk. *Divergent Lines* had been an unnecessary ball-and-chain to his creativity, along with all the other excuses he had made up over the past ten years. That was enough procrastination.

He looked at the charred but still readable hardcover of *Infernities*. First, before he started on any new book or short story, he had to write a letter.

"Dear Mr. Cardiff, let me make you a bargain." He proposed that if he had not produced any new novels or short stories in the next five years, then Jeremy had his blessing to publish *Infernities*, if only to reward the fans who had waited so long. He packaged the letter with the scorched book and mailed it to his "number one fan." Simply knowing the novel existed would be all the inspiration he really needed.

On the way back from the mailbox, he smiled to himself, convinced it would never be necessary for the other Mitchell Coren's book to be published here. He would take that risk for himself.

About the Author

Kevin J. Anderson has published 140 books, 54 of which have been national or international bestsellers. He has written numerous novels in the Star Wars, X-Files, and Dune universes, as well as unique steampunk fantasy novels *Clockwork Angels* and *Clockwork Lives*, written with legendary rock drummer Neil Peart, based on the concept album by the band Rush. His original works include the Saga of Seven Suns series, the Terra Incognita fantasy trilogy, the Saga of Shadows trilogy, and his humorous horror series featuring Dan Shamble, Zombie PI. He has edited numerous anthologies, written comics and games, and the lyrics to two rock CDs. Anderson and his wife Rebecca Moesta are the publishers of WordFire Press.

If You Liked ...

If you liked *Alternitech*, you might also enjoy:

Blindfold
Hopscotch
Climbing Olympus

Other WordFire Press Titles

Our list of other WordFire Press authors and titles is always growing. To find out more and to see our selection of titles, visit us at:

wordfirepress.com

* 9 7 8 1 6 1 4 7 5 0 6 5 9 *